The Flying Hart

Stories by Claire Macquet

Sheba Feminist Publishers

First published in 1991 by Sheba Feminist Publishers,
10a Bradbury St, London N16 8JN.

Copyright © Claire Macquet 1991

All rights reserved.

No part of this book may be reproduced or transmitted in any form or by any means, electronic or mechanical, in whole or in part (except brief quotations for purpose of review), without prior permission in writing from Sheba Feminist Publishers.

Cover illustration and design by Catherine Arthur

Typeset by Dale Gunthorp

Printed and bound in the UK by Cox & Wyman Ltd, Reading

British Library Cataloguing in Publication Data

> Macquet, Claire
> The flying hart
> I. Title
> 823.914 [F]
>
> ISBN 0-907179-55-X

'Mondi' was first published in *Critical Quarterly*, 1989.
'Gypsophila' appeared in *In and Out of Time*, Onlywomen Press, 1990

Claire Macquet's first novel, *Looking for Ammu*, is to be published by Virago in 1992.

Acknowledgements:
I owe special thanks to Lilian Mohin and Anna Livia, for much helpful advice and criticism. Also to C.V. McCarthy, and the members of my writing group, in particular, Barbara Gough. To Sheba: Michelle McKenzie and Sue O'Sullivan, my diligent and ever patient editors, and Araba Mercer, source of a million marketing and production ideas, grateful thanks.

for Catherine
for always

Contents

The Baboon's Stepladder p 1
Miss Vandyk's Game p 21
Gypsophila p 31
Sparrow p 44
Mondi p 59
After the Party p 68
Overnighting at De Aar p 78
Night at the Rana's Palace p 90
Jonquil p 101
Jo-Soap's Last Gift p 113
The Hockey Club p 123
A World Apart p 129
The Magdalen at Forty p 144

Queen and huntress, chaste and fair...

*Lay thy bow of pearl apart,
And thy crystal-shining quiver;
Give unto the flying hart
Space to breathe, how short soever
Thou that mak'st a day of night—
Goddess excellently bright.*

Ben Jonson

The Baboon's Stepladder

Ferocious barking split the night. Sarie jumped; something caught at her hair: '*Voetsak!*'

'Easy, easy now,' muttered an unfamiliar voice beside her. 'It's only baboons.'

Sarie untangled her hair from the rough fabric of the tent and slid back inside the sleeping bag. She made herself small as a child, not touching the bodies on either side, lying still until her heartbeat eased to a regular thump. Only baboons!

The barking was now broken by howls, somewhere close; closer still, in the grass that sprang like wire out of the rocks, there was a rustling — baboons sniffing the remains of their *braaivleis*? scorpions? night adders?

'Estelle' — in a cautious whisper — 'is the tent zipped up against snakes?'

'You wanna suffocate? Get some sleep; you'll need to be fresh to climb mountains tomorrow.'

'Sorry.'

Sarie bunched her fists. She couldn't do one thing right. She hurt nobody; why then was everything that breathed so horrible to her? She tried. She was trying now: getting away from Koos Steenkamp who had betrayed her; being friends with the woman who had made it happen. She lay stiffly, ignoring the prickles all over her skin, telling her body it was out here in the Magaliesberg Mountains, where you feel free.

She jumped again when Estelle's arm landed like an animal on her chest. 'You'll get used to the bush in a while,' came the sleepy voice again. 'It's safer than crossing Buurmansdorp Main Street. And a lot safer than being anywhere near that Steenkamp.'

'Okay. Sorry I woke you.'

Estelle was already asleep again. And at least Faan hadn't wakened. Sarie lay till dawn, thinking how sad it was that at the age of only twenty-two, in the year of 1965 when progress was at last beginning to nibble at the fringes of the Transvaal Platteland, she had ruined her life. Sad too to know that the tears that dribbled into her ears would turn her eyes into boggy puddles by morning — another bitter little tribute to Estelle!

They were up shortly after five, in a pale peachy windless light that bleached their faces but left untouched the deep night in the ravine. Faan especially, with her staring cheekbones, looked much older — you could just imagine her at thirty. She had gone off, Sarie thought at first to reconnoitre, but had been ages standing at the edge of the ravine — throwing a shadow almost as long as those rock piles that loomed like the idols of some heathen god — gazing into the dawn; praying maybe; with Faan you could never tell.

The rocks, the spiny, hunchbacked bushes, the withered aloes, that pink light. It was all very strange. Strangest of all was the emptiness, in which the sound of breathing, hard in the thin air, seemed to evaporate.

Being inside the mountains was quite different from looking at them from the national road to Mafeking — not exactly disappointing, Sarie thought, just different. From there they were definite, ranks of koppies behind the cosmos flowers. Inside (not on top, because there was no one point) they were a huge shapeless sprawl of rubble, without any sense or direction, as in a city abandoned after an earthquake. In here, there was nothing to tell that it was September, springtime. There was no soil. There were no paths, no farms, no people. Nothing grew that was not dry and spiny. You could sense the pulse somewhere of life, of scaly things in crevices with no language but stings and poison. There was nothing that creatures could eat except each other.

This, then, was the world as God had made it and perhaps intended it to stay. Sarie was thoughtful. She looked carefully at Faan's long silhouette, then at Estelle and wondered quite why it had seemed so apt to put herself at the mercy of this hard woman who had brought about her downfall.

Estelle was boiling maize porridge over a little fire. Sarie popped the deodorant stick back into her handbag and went up to her. 'Can I do anything?'

She was set to rolling up the sleeping bags and stacking them, beside their food stores, in the rafters of the tent (against insects). Estelle certainly liked to give orders. Then to packing a bag with plenty of suncream, dried fruit and biscuits. This made her feel better.

'The climb we're going to do today,' she asked, 'is it very steep?'

'No, more of a scramble really; down the ravine and up a little cliff we call the Baboon's Stepladder.' Estelle tasted the porridge and plunged the spoon straight back into the pot. 'There's a waterfall up there. On a shelf near the top it tips into a pool so deep we've never touched the bottom.'

'Is that where the baboons were last night?'

'Could be, they move about. They'll probably be round the camp when we're gone.'

'Will they be here when we get back?'

'I hope not. We'll leave it clean, no scraps of food about. They can be dangerous.'

'Have you got a gun?'

Estelle laughed. 'I'm glad Faan didn't hear you say that. Remember, the baboons live here.'

'Sorry.'

'But if the Stepladder bothers you, we'll rope you up.'

Sarie bristled. 'I don't need any rope, thanks.'

'Yes, you'll be fine.' Estelle poured half a packet of sugar into the porridge. It was a mystery how she stayed so slim. And even out here in this wilderness her head was sleek and glossy as someone on the bioscope, though nobody — not even Elizabeth Taylor — had features as fine. No wonder Koos Steenkamp had fallen for her and only turned to Sarie in his despair. Sarie measured her pale, plump arms against Estelle's brown ones, curving away from slender shoulders, and grimaced at the absurdity.

'Call Faan for breakfast, will you, or she'll be standing there all day.'

Sarie hobbled across the rocks to alert Faan by a touch to the sleeve. In this place, it didn't seem right to shout.

The Magaliesberg are not very important mountains, just a broken-backed ridge on the high plateau of the Witwatersrand. Sarie grew up in Zeerust, quite nearby in African terms, but she'd never seen them except from the road. Zeerust regarded the mountains as a waste land, of interest only to youths venturing into the fringes to shoot baboons.

Anyway, the family always took their holidays by the sea, at Umkomaas. This was the decade when cars became reliable and roads passable even after summer storms, when Transvaalers who were not rich could discover the seaside. Once the family had detoured on the way home, driving up to Champagne Castle in the High Drakensberg, where giant sweeps of black and ochre rock soared out of the valleys into the upper reaches of a heaven hard as lapis lazuli, and a lamergeyer had wheeled high above their picnic. Her mother's arm was about Sarie's shoulder in the photograph that showed both their mouths stretched in smiles, their eyes screwed tight against the light, orange squash and sandwiches glinting on the little roadside table before them. Perhaps this picture, still living those virgin days before Koos, had persuaded Sarie to take up Estelle's offer of a weekend's escape to the mountains.

Why not? They had things in common, the three young women. They were the new intake at the Provincial Administration depot in Buurmansdorp, all put to translating reports from Afrikaans into English and back. They all needed a year's experience in the provinces to get jobs in Pretoria; they belonged to the same church, and they were drafted together into the hockey club. They all worked under the handsome, soulful Meneer Steenkamp, the only eligible bachelor in Buurmansdorp who was not a rugby-playing farmer.

What is more, they were none of them, now not even Sarie, much to Buurmansdorp's taste. With that tight-mouthed discretion that is raised to an art form on the Platteland, Buurmansdorp bore their presence with stoicism.

Faan had a fine old Dutch name, but her broad face and hair cropped down to its grizzly roots hinted that she was not as white as a van der Stel ought to be. But, unlike the van Rooyens, Erasmuses and other perhaps tainted Boer families, she didn't shuffle into church and squeeze into a back pew. With a ripple of unease, Buurmansdorp followed her movements as, like a long, dark shadow cast by the brilliance of Estelle, Faan followed her friend up to the Communion table. As they watched her, lips unmoving even during the National Anthem, the burgers were relieved that she stayed away from their sons and daughters. There was something gross and immodest about her, even in her silences: everybody knew though nobody mentioned the shocking ways she sometimes broke them.

Estelle of the gazelle's body and violet eyes disturbed them almost as much: she was too beautiful for a quiet town. The madness that had afflicted poor Steenkamp was proof to all how dangerous such a thing could be.

As they walked down the dusty main street, Estelle closely followed by Faan, Buurmansdorp, peering from behind lace curtains, complained that Estelle's heels were too high, her laugh too loud, her skirts too full and flowery; that Faan was too tall, her hands and feet too big for a virtuous woman. The real causes of offence were not mentioned.

With Sarie it was different — or had been at the beginning. Sarie was a local girl. In his youth, long before he rose to prominence, the Burgermeester had courted her mother, riding horseback to Zeerust with the gift of half a sheep or a porridge spoon carved out of assegaiwood. Everyone with a spare room had been ready to offer Sarie lodgings, and to chat to her over breakfast about the old days when cooking pots were polished until they shone like mirrors. Then Sarie had done that thing to Steenkamp. They hadn't needed to hear the worst from Koos himself; from the start her behaviour towards him had been excitable, strumpish.

Yet Sarie knew she would never have stepped out of line to claim Koos Steenkamp for herself had he not been brought so low by Estelle's cruelty to him. Sarie had never before seen a woman crush a man as if he were a cockroach. Nor had she seen a grown man cry. At first appalled by the sobs that broke like painful hiccups out of the depths of his body, when she discovered that she loved him, she felt his pain in her own.

It had started one Saturday, at the town hall social (Estelle was in the mountains with Faan of course — another of the shockingly unwomanly things they did). Sarie had taken advantage of the Leap Year dance to draw Koos onto the floor and into her arms to dance to Jan Pierewit:

> 'Good morning my wife,
> Here's a little kiss for life;'
> 'Good morning my man,
> There is coffee in the pan.'
> Jan Pierewit, stand still.

'I know how you feel about Estelle,' she whispered into his ear as her Jan Pierewit, obeying orders, crashed to a halt, 'and I pity you with all my heart.'

Afterwards Koos had taken her to his lodgings, and thrust into her hand a sheaf of poems to Estelle. Sarie had never been inside a bachelor's quarters before, and found herself shocked by the flipped-up lavatory seat, the row of sinister little bottles above the washbasin, the glimpse of bedding pulled tight as a shroud, the sour smell of tobacco in the study. Koos was different here: breath running hard through the hairs in his nostrils, smelling of his tweed jacket, he was foreign and frightening. But she sat to read the verses, odes in the style of Goethe; she had never known poetry to have such power, never known her nerves to behave so like a flock of birds ready to scatter to the winds at the first footfall.

She had shown the poems to her mother at Sunday lunch in Zeerust, hoping that Mammie would be as moved as she was by their deep pathos. Her mother had glanced briefly at the neat italic hand and said, 'Remember *dogtertjie*, how important it is to keep a man's respect.'

That message even a good girl could forget, even in orderly Buurmansdorp, kissing away his tears in a corner of the car park one lunch hour, her stomach inching closer till it just brushed the knob below his long stomach. She forgot lots. She forgot that men hate being chased and put bunches of zinnias on his desk. She forgot her modesty, even, when he kissed her back, dreaming for a moment that Estelle might be ousted. She forgot her manners and wished Estelle old and ugly. And then she forgot her morals and late one night, after she had given him Estelle's message ('*Voetsak!*') she put Meneer Steenkamp's hand in the place no girl should ever put a man's hand.

This hadn't, none the less, been quite what it seemed; Buurmansdorp had been cruel in its judgment. Sarie was not one of those women who couldn't wait until they got engaged; she knew how to be chaste, even in her daydreams. It happened because of Estelle.

Sometimes, when Sarie sat at her work, trying to recall the English phrase for 'congruity of interests' or something of the like, she would catch sight of Estelle's pen flowing smoothly over the paper, and she knew that its phrases would be as perfect as the slender fingers that shaped them. And then a hot needle would pierce her side, drive to her heart, in a pain so sudden and sharp she feared she would cry out. She could have found some relief if Estelle had ever had some small imperfection — just once a bee-sting on her forehead, a touch of sunburn, mud on the hem of her skirt — but all of nature was her servant. And then Sarie would run to Koos willing to die if that could help him bear such a terrible love.

Yes, she would say, she would take his messages; she would carry to Estelle the lovingly-wrapped recording of Mahler's Fifth Symphony, knowing that Estelle would scorn the gift and that Sarie would burn with the shame of Koos's shame when she took the record back to him.

And so it had happened that Sarie, trying to help, trying to assuage both their feelings, had gone again to his lodgings and held him until he, suddenly frantic, had, hard and hasty, taken her. Afterwards, drenched in sweat, he had turned away his head and wept that Sarie had defiled the purity of his love.

That way she had lost his respect. And as he, who told all the world about his desperate passion, also told of this, she lost everyone's respect. The chemist picked up the coins she had touched with his handkerchief. In the street, the rugby club howled after her like a pack of dogs. At church, the dominie put his hand in his pocket when she reached out to take it.

She said nothing to defend herself. She knew nobody could understand that she wanted to do something, give him something of great value, something that would make him feel a man again. And so she had given him her downfall: perhaps, at the telling of it, he had felt a man again. In that thought, she took a bitter pleasure. She was utterly alone. She wanted to be alone. Love was a pain you could die of. Sometimes, looking at her body in the mirror, she marvelled at it, made transparent by love. Before, she had seen it as porky, unfinished, sluglike. Now she felt a tenderness for its soft young curves, and she pitied it for being appreciated by nobody but herself. Sometimes, too, she thought of the deep passion that had burst from it, and it crossed her mind that Koos's love for Estelle was manmade and theatrical compared with hers for him.

Nobody but she knew how grand and wounded a soul walked the dusty streets of Buurmansdorp. But from Faan came an uncouth perhaps sympathy that filled Sarie with dread.

Estelle and Faan had turned up at Communion soon after. That Sunday, the sermon was torture for Sarie. 'The chastity of women,' said the dominie, 'is the foundation of morality. On it depends the family, the state, the race — all order.' Sarie, head bent, heard a rustling — figures turning, she was sure, to stare at her. 'Chastity' (another rustling as attention was recalled to the pulpit) 'is woman's gift to civilization.'

Head still bent, Sarie stood, sat, kneeled; and then left, hard on the heels of Estelle, Faan shadowing. On the steps of the vestibule, Faan had paused, grasped the dominie's hand and said, in her clear Cape voice: 'It would solve the problem of chastity if God tied men's balls around their necks.' Sarie still couldn't bear to think about that thing that Faan had said.

Nor did she want to think of how her isolation had laid her open to the cold violet eyes of the woman who could watch another woman fall without herself being in any danger: they showed something that was not contempt for Sarie but in a way something worse.

Koos Steenkamp, forced to do his own courting now that his go-between was disgraced, came more often, timidly, into their office. One day he slipped a note into Estelle's in-tray. 'Take that thing away, Steenkamp,' Estelle called without looking up; 'I'll not touch the droppings of a rat.' Poor Koos had picked up the folded sheet of paper and gone quietly out of the room. These things too Sarie didn't want to think about.

Yet she knew that that way Estelle kept her slave, trod him down to where Sarie was. Her mother, had she read of such a thing in a story, would have said 'Of course *dogtertjie*, what would you expect?'

All Buurmansdorp was talking. Sarie was mute. Estelle and Faan too never spoke of the thing; they showed that it mattered in an awful kindness. When the farmers' sons whistled at Sarie all down the street, Faan would yell: 'You oafs want the feel of my *sjambok*?' And Estelle would softly say: 'Come Sarie, walk with Faan and me.'

And that's how it happened that, after they had eaten their porridge like animals — without conversation, pausing only to sniff the wind — Sarie sat in that swept lunar landscape with the arm Koos so longed to touch draped around her shoulder. She was trying on Estelle's spare climbing boots. Fit perfect; made her ankles feel strong as horses' hooves. Estelle smiled approval. Sarie tested against the rock the grip of deeply incised rubber soles that Koos would have given his life to kiss.

The soles bit into softness when they dropped into the ravine — Faan first, then Sarie, Estelle close behind — releasing smells of warm moist earth. The dense scrub closed over their heads and it was another world, filled with birdcalls, the scuttle of creatures in the leaves, a whisper of water. You could breathe. Faan paused every now and then to examine a fungus or a flower, name a bird from the flash of its plumage or an insect from its click, to test a rock. Sarie's feet were light in Estelle's boots. Her hands braced themselves easily against springy ivy-clad stems.

Her heart that had closed tight up on the rocks eased a little, letting in first joy and then a surge of grief that there should be such a lovely, secret place to be with Koos. As Faan pointed out peaty pockets where dassies slept, Sarie saw how sweetly this earth would cradle Estelle's slender shoulders should the princess design to lie there with the only possible lover.

Half an hour's scrambling at a pace measurable by the steadily rising sound of water brought them down to the stream, surprisingly dainty to make such a racket; another hour or so along the thickety bottom, with scarcely a glimpse of the sky, to a cliff, where they paused, and splashed their faces.

It had been chilly up on the rocks. Here it was hot and close. As she washed the smears of half a dozen cuts from her arms and legs, and waited patiently for the stinging to subside, Sarie became aware of a headache. Faan was lying on her stomach, sucking water straight out of the stream like an animal. Estelle came over and sat down beside Sarie: still glossy as a film star, she wasn't even out of breath.

Sarie noted the long brown legs that stretched out, so smooth, so relaxed — so full of themselves — and recalled herself to herself with a wash of rage: to her that hath had been given and given and given until she was so stuffed up with fortune that she would not even bother to see how cruel was her kindness to a creature so far beneath her. Nor how mean to Sarie was the pleasure she took in torturing Koos. She had such power that she could have given him to Sarie, had she cared to. It was so unfair: the princess had everything to herself, including the thing she didn't want but Sarie wanted more than all the world.

Estelle's hand was on her arm. 'Nice here isn't it? No spies from the Provincial Administration.'

Sarie started at the touch. 'No,' she said, then, uncertainly, 'Well, it's really nice, really wild, but if you died here, nobody would know.' They wouldn't die, she thought, they belong here. But I could die now and Koos wouldn't even want to know.

Faan lifted her head from the water. 'God would know,' she called, 'and it's nobody else's business.'

Something very like a chill wind enclosed Sarie — those bleak broken tombstones up top, this steamy grave-bottom —

Faan and Estelle were not like normal people. Help, she whispered to herself.

She thought hard. 'Really, that wasn't what I meant,' she said quickly, 'But, you see — well — they're real nature, these mountains; but they're not beautiful.' She thought, with a pang, of the photograph in the Drakensberg. No, these mountains were not beautiful. They were misshapen, derelict; they were, perhaps, like her love for Koos, like the friendship of these two women. O help me, she thought. I am so alone.

'You think Buurmansdorp is beautiful?' snorted Estelle.

Faan chipped in. 'That's not what Sarie said.'

Sarie struggled. 'Well, perhaps, really, they are beautiful. But they don't mean anything.' That was closer to it. 'They just go round and round,' she added, 'like the planets.' Round and round, she thought, like being in love with a man who will never love you, not till the end of the world.

'No doubt,' Estelle was still sharp, 'people will make them mean something. They'll send fishermen to this stream soon, then dam the ravine for a hydroelectric power station. When they do,' she added bitterly, 'they'll have to shoot Faan along with the baboons.'

'Oh no!' Sarie was mortified. 'I was only trying to say that I don't feel I belong here; I can't get in tune with it. It's my fault; that's all I meant.'

'You meant what you said.' Faan's long form was looming. 'And you're right. They don't mean anything. Why should they? Were they made to decorate your philosophy?'

O help, Sarie whispered again.

'Don't give her all that,' Estelle snapped at Faan, and, gently, said to Sarie: 'Look at this *bekkie*, so small and clear, yet it cut this great ravine. It comes from the top,' she pointed, 'tips into the little pool and disappears into the rock. It comes out again, here, at the bottom of the cliff. It's still cutting, you see, into the ravine. One day this whole face will peel away, and the rock will fall to where we're sitting now.'

'I also did geography at school,' Sarie muttered glumly.

'Yes, but did you taste the water?' Estelle's fingers lightly laced themselves with Sarie's, slipping silkily against skin that had burned in the grasp of Koos's palms. 'Taste now, see how pure it is.'

Sarie's mouth was dry. 'I'm not thirsty.'

Estelle's hand moved away, leaving Sarie's surprised, orphaned. 'Well, really I am thirsty,' Sarie added, 'but I don't know if it's safe to drink downstream of the baboons.'

Estelle's hand came back. 'Baboons wouldn't mess their own drinking water; they're not like humans. I'll get you some to taste; you'll see.'

Sarie drank water that was cupped in two long, beautiful hands; its purity she couldn't judge, her senses stunned by the feel of the fine skin that her lips reached down to. Her body began to throb a little, the soft start of its drumbeat call for Koos — Koos cultivating his despair, heavy as a storm-cloud, reaching out to touch, and turning everything limp. If only she could make him listen, make him look, unlock to him these mountains, this water, this hand, Faan's words to empower his poems.

She looked up into eyes brighter than the sky. Something — something — didn't mean nothing. She reached for it. 'Estelle,' she said, 'I'm still in love with Koos.'

'Yes.'

'I'm jealous of you.'

'I know.'

'I've wished you dead, often.'

'Of course.'

How could she say she didn't wish Estelle dead now? 'I wish you wouldn't be so cruel to him.'

'Well then, stop me, you little donkey. You tell him what a miserable worm he is, and spare me the trouble.'

'People can love worms,' said Faan.

Sarie was delighted. 'That's right. I do.'

'But they don't have to squirm with them,' said Estelle.

'Why not? A squirm is just another way of moving.'

'Come on, Faan,' Estelle rounded hotly. 'You know perfectly well what I mean. Sarie's letting that slob humiliate her, and thinking it's part of some deep experience. Next time round she'll be looking for a beating-up man.'

Sarie was fierce. 'I won't be looking for anyone. I'm going to save Koos.'

'I hope you succeed,' said Faan.

'Kick him in the arse first.'

Sarie looked up into Estelle's flushed face. 'Okay,' she said. If you will be my friend, she added in thought, I can do just that.

The face was tall and sheer as the Provincial Administration block. The stone, its pale granite blackened with moisture at the bottom and burnt almost white near the top, was laid neatly in metre-wide blocks, laced with strong grey vines. Sarie had been quite good at climbing trees once. She took comfort from the powerful vines.

'Perfect climb, isn't it?' Estelle was half-shouting against the noise of the water, very loud here.

Sarie nodded. She looked up towards the top, far above her.

'We found it last winter; you could see more of it then. Come.' Estelle led her by the hand to the face. 'Take your handholds at the clean rock,' she said into Sarie's ear, 'And put your feet there. Beware of the greenery.'

'Of course.' Sarie now noticed that the vines held with little hair-thin roots about two centimetres long, clumped like spiders. She shuddered.

'Always look up; best don't look at anything except Faan's bottom. Say if you want us to rope you up.'

She could so easily have said she wouldn't do it. She could wait for them to go up to the wonderful little waterfall on the shelf and come down again. She didn't have to look at Faan's bottom. It would only be sensible to say she was afraid.

'I'll be right behind you, so if you need to fall, you can fall on me.'

Sarie turned to the violet eyes.

'I'm glad you're here,' Estelle said seriously. 'Nobody knows this place except Faan and me, and I always wanted to show it somebody, somebody we could trust not to tell.'

Estelle was close. Sarie smelled her sweat. Koos would not have admired that smell. Koos could not have followed her here. Sarie was glad she was going to do it.

Faan's old-fashioned, wide-legged shorts hung above her like sails. Sarie's heart was steadier now. She had taken on several ridges, and nothing had gone wrong. Her fingers had shown skill at selecting holds; her feet in Estelle's boots had gone direct to crevices her eyes hadn't been aware of; the strength in her arms had surprised her, so had the length of her reach; her whole body felt long and supple; every part was thinking for itself and sending messages of triumph and encouragement buzzing down the nerves to every other part. Her breath was singing to the full-throated pump of her blood. Close up, she saw that even the white rock was home to delicate patches of lichen, cool against her cheek. It was the vines now which looked sinister, twisting close into the rock, soft and treacherous against its dry firmness. The waterfall was closer, yet its bubbling had retreated to an infinite distance. She felt vague pains here and there, but they were of no consequence.

They crossed from the shadow into clean sunshine. One move at a time she advanced into the bright light, her hands creeping upward for the next grip.

A corner of her eye caught the swing of Faan's legs, out into space, and gone. Faan was on the ledge with the pool so deep nobody had ever touched the bottom. Sarie was nearly there. The friend who trusted her was just below.

As she drew herself over the belly of the next ridge, rock came away in her hand. What?

What? Why were both her hands around a stem of vine? 'Help!'

With a whistle like a long whip, a piece of vine above her head unpeeled itself from the face and streaked down, out of sight. The chunk of rock was gone. She must have dropped it. Sarie hung on, panting. 'Help!'

The stem in her hands slipped a little, so that she lost her footholds, but then it tightened and held, and the boots scrabbled for new support.

'No!' It was Estelle from below, 'Hold the rock!'

The vine was firm now, though Sarie's position was not quite vertical. Anyway, her limbs were paralysed. She grinned. 'Estelle. I think I'm stuck.'

'Faan!'

'Faan, Faan, Faan.' The ravine echoed Estelle's call.

Sarie glanced down to see if an avalanche was starting. Her heart jumped to note the level earth so great a distance below. She looked away. There had been a red thing like a squashed tomato on Estelle's forehead. The piece of rock must have hit her. She could hear Faan on the cliff. Her hands were numb, glued to the vine. The hands that had been so clever before now refused to release the thin grey stem. She saw the torn ends of root hairs, clear as under a magnifying glass, and laid her cheek against them. They felt like the stubble on Koos's chin. The vine slipped another few inches. She turned her face to it, pressing her mouth against its rough skin, a last kiss; a gift she hadn't expected.

'Oh Koos,' she whispered, 'I know you are a shallow, weak man. But it never mattered. I should have told you it didn't matter. I know you don't love me, but that too never mattered.' Sad as they were, these things, even their sadness didn't matter.

She felt Estelle's hand, placing a foot, that seemed to be dangling, on somewhere. Estelle should go away. Estelle was the most beautiful person in the world. Sarie didn't want to bring her down when the vine gave. She felt Faan's hand, stringing a rope under her arms. 'I'll be all right, thank you Faan.' Faan should go away; 'Just catching my breath.' But Sarie didn't resist when Faan prised the fingers of one of her hands from the creeper and hung them, like four little coathanger hooks, onto a ridge of rock. Such pretty fingers, so sweet and sad with their nails all broken.

Faan was up at the top again. She could swarm over the cliff quick as a monkey. The rope tightened across Sarie's chest. She made no effort to help, not even looking as Estelle moved her feet, wooden puppets in the boots, lifting and pushing them here and there; her brain — stiff as her limbs — knew only mild shock as she was hauled up to the rim and then over onto the sloping surface of the ledge.

Then limbs that had been so clever and then so stupid, jerked back to life, and she crawled frantically into the deepest corner.

She stuck her head between her knees, and wrapped her arms around her poor self, shuffling in tight. The whole thing became clear: she had nearly died; she had nearly died. And if she had, nobody would ever love Koos.

But where were her friends, her friends who had saved her?

'Faan?' There was the little waterfall. There was the pool. Above her more cliff. Before her, a short slope down to the void. No Faan, no Estelle. Oh my God, she thought, the rock. The rock she had dropped. Dropped on Estelle's head. Flat on her stomach, she slithered towards the edge. It wasn't very far. 'Faan?'

Forcing her eyes to open she looked out into space, and then, stomach dropping, looked down. Hanging on the cliff, pressed up into the vines, were two heads, spokes of arms. Estelle, pressed up against the rockface, Faan's body around and over her, like spiders.

'Faan!' Sarie shouted loud over the racket of the waterfall. 'Faan! Is Estelle hurt?'

Faan looked up. As her head tilted back, Sarie caught of a glimpse of Estelle's forehead. Blood. Lots of blood.

'I'll help. I'm coming down. Just hold her.' Her breath rattling, Sarie turned round, and lowered a shaking foot towards the first crack, her hands searching the smooth sloping surface of the ledge for something to grasp.

'Sarie!' Faan was shouting too. 'Don't try that. Get the rope.'

What rope? Oh yes, the rope. One end was still around her chest. She swivelled back to face the cliff, pulling in the other end. It was wet. It must have been in the pool. She dropped it down over the edge. 'Grab it, Faan,' she shouted.

'No, we'd just pull you over. Wind it round something firm, that big rock near the waterfall, and hold the end.'

Sarie looked back. A big embedded rock, but too far to reach. Quickly, think quickly. It would reach if she loosened it from her chest. She struggled with the loop. Help! Faan must be getting tired. Rope wouldn't loosen. Do something quickly. Yes: She could be the something firm. Her boots could reach the lip of the pool, grip its edge, smoothly undercut by the little waterfall. The rope could stay around her chest; she would become part of it, hooked by her instep, encased in Estelle's hard leather, to the pool. She dropped the rope over the edge again. 'It's firm now Faan.'

'Sure? Right round the rock? Test it one more time.'

'It's firm. You pull.'

The rope tightened like a vice, pushing the breath out of her body; sending a pain shooting to her knee as it crushed the tendon in her instep; but her feet were iron.

'We're coming up now.'

Sarie couldn't breathe, couldn't speak.

Slowly, slowly, Faan grunting like a hog, her long body still spread over Estelle's, they edged closer. The rope slackened. Sarie pulled it in, twisted it, tighter than a tourniquet, round her upper arm. Another shuffle upwards. One metre now from the ledge. Oh help, please! Sarie pulled in more rope. The other end was around Estelle's chest. They were tied, she and the beautiful Estelle, like Siamese twins. Estelle's hands were feebly catching at rocks, vines, the rope. Faan grunted, her teeth fastened into the back of Estelle's shirt.

Sarie pulled harder. Her feet, completely numb from the press against the lip and coldness of the water yet still firm as meathooks, dug deeper into the pool. Half a metre. Sarie, both arms now trussed with the rope, could not reach down. Oh help, please help!

Then Faan's powerful wonderful brown hand reached up and grasped the edge of the shelf. Another heave. Inches from Sarie's, Estelle's head appeared. On her shockingly white forehead was a long gash, the bone showing through, like a great grinning mouth.

'Hello there, Sarie,' said Estelle.

They dragged her up to the corner, and laid her gently down. The rucksack was gone; baboons would find the dried peaches and biscuits and the first aid kit at the bottom of the cliff. Faan washed the wound from the pool, whipped off her shirt, tore it into strips and bandaged Estelle's head. Then she pulled off her shorts and wrapped them around Estelle's shoulders.

Sarie did nothing useful. She was holding Estelle's hand, thinking of the beautiful face which had become monstrous. 'I'm so sorry; I'm so sorry, Estelle.'

Estelle smiled. 'Why? You were wonderful with the rope: did everything possible wrong, and got the answer right.'

'Faan:' Sarie turned to the tall form, trying not be shocked at the sight of adult female nakedness, 'It was me. I dropped that rock. That rock that hit Estelle.'

'Did you?' Faan said vaguely. 'I suppose you feel bad about that.' Faan was looking up towards the lip of the ravine. 'Estelle might get the rest of the way up to the top if we both helped her, don't you think?'

Sarie winced at the thought of Estelle, so peaceful now, forced back into danger; of Faan climbing, the rock rasping her bare breasts. 'I'll help. I'll do whatever you say.'

'Then we'd have to get down to the van Rensburg farm. They could fetch the district nurse to put in some stitches. But it's about ten kilometres to the farm. A bit too far, I think.'

'I'll carry her. I want to carry her.'

Estelle laughed. 'That'd be nice.'

'I think,' said Faan, 'it's best I go for help. You wait here with Estelle.'

Sarie's heart leapt. 'All right. Here, take my clothes.'

'Keep them. You'll need them to give Estelle more cover when the sun goes.'

'That's all right.' Sarie would give Estelle the cover of her own body. She would hold her in her arms like a lover. She would keep her warm with her own life. She had not unbuttoned her blouse with such joy when she did it for Koos.

Then a thought struck her. 'No, Faan. That's not right. I should go. Estelle needs you more than me. She loves you more than me.'

'It's dangerous. If you fell on one of the climbs, nobody would find you.'

'I won't fall.'

'What happens to Estelle if you get lost?'

'Tell me the way.'

'And it's harder still to find the way back. If there's a wait at the farm it might be night.'

'I'll get back. I know I can do it. Tell me what to do.'

'Let Sarie do it,' said Estelle.

Sarie ran at the cliff like a dassie and was over the top in no time. Nor would she lose her way to the farm. As Faan had instructed, she stopped often to note the route, almost due south allowing for the northerly angle of the sun at this spring equinox. And, as instructed, she adjusted the image for a sun which would have wheeled round to the other side, or gone, by the time of her return, for outcrops of rock which would change their profile, looked at from a different angle. There were definite features: the ribbon of green marking the edge of the ravine, the fan of taller bush fed by the waterfall, the long belly of stone broken by one thorn tree, the anthill beneath.

She ran, walked, crawled; wherever she could, she broke into a lope whose rhythm masked the stitch in her side, the waves of faintness from thirst and hunger and a broiling sun. Along one stretch, a troupe of about six baboons paced her, two with babies riding piggypack. They ran along on all fours, rising up from time to time to check her progress. She marvelled at their tirelessness, their speed. She longed to speak their language, beg them to hurry on to the farm; to take the message ahead of her, tell them that Estelle had not fallen when the rock struck her. Because Sarie was her friend and trusted her, Estelle had waited; Estelle had saved Sarie's life before she was willing to receive the force of the wound.

Sarie hadn't known it before; she was a native of these parts. She barely needed Faan's directions. '*Bobbejaantjies*,' she found the breath to shout at them: 'Koos Steenkamp couldn't love Estelle more than I do.' And then she laughed as their heads popped up, then down, and their tails curved high above them as they bounded ahead.

By mid afternoon, Sarie was on the return, still scrambling, loping and striding, with Meneer van Rensberg (of the Buurmansdorp rugby club) and his son, carrying blankets and a stretcher.

They reached the ledge before dark. Estelle's head was cradled in Faan's breast. Sarie felt a pang — it could have been her breast — but she was proud to have done the right thing, and done it well. Van Rensberg looked away respectfully as Sarie covered both her friends with blankets.

'What a lotta fuss,' said Estelle thickly. 'I'm okay, just wanna get back to the camp.'

They carried Estelle back by starlight, the Southern Cross guiding them to the farm where, by now, the district nurse would be boiling his needle and catgut in the kettle. In the distance, they heard baboons barking, perhaps swarming a camp where there was food in the rafters of the tent. It didn't matter; nor would the scar that Estelle would now wear for life make her any less beautiful.

Miss Vandyk's Game

Judy Pilgrim called the temp 'Miss Vandyk' even though she knew perfectly well her name was Veronica. Why not? She wasn't paid to pretend she liked her.

So what if she drew fire in return, getting called 'Mistress Pilgrim'.

So what if, on Veronica's tea days, that great lout of a Sloane Ranger let out in a parrot's screech: 'Would Mistress Pilgrim like her coffee black, with cream, with strawberries?' Judy loathed coffee anyway — stuff that smelled like sump-oil — and fifteen years in England was time enough to be hardened to the mocking of smart white people.

'Sticks and stones may break my bones but laughter never hurt me.' So, Miss Veronica Vandyk was somebody because she was the daugher of Mrs Veronica Vandyk who was the daughter of another great white lady. Judith Pilgrim, daughter of nobody much, from Dominica (a country that to English people existed only in the cruel fictions of Jean Rhys), needed to be somebody to no one but herself. It was a self that didn't want patronage thank you from the world's sloppiest filing clerk.

That great institution, the National Industrial Policy Institute (NIPI for short), without which the British economy would instantly collapse, had employed Judy Pilgrim, clerk, for a decade. She had started out on the filing Miss Vandyk now so mismanaged, then, after taking a computer course at night school, moved on to coding and feeding into the new computer statistics on the wool textile industry. She had written some minor (and later some not so minor) adjustments into the program to make it easier for the other dumbcluck clerks to operate. She was, however, still paid as a filing clerk. So what if NIPI's recent acquisitions, graduates in computer science, got twice her pay; they still had to turn to Judy to solve the problems.

So Veronica Vandyk could scrape no skin off her nose. Nor need she bother to tell Miss Vandyk that it was tedious always having to search for statistical reports which had been filed, if at all, under 'memoranda' or 'expenses' or something equally stupid.

One day, while Judy was searching for just such a file, while Veronica watched her, legs looped over the arm of her chair, Veronica said: 'What's the first thing comes into your head when you wake up in the morning?'

Judy started. She should have said 'Mind your own business', but she didn't — too busy asking herself what was in her head. Was it that she ought to say her prayers but wouldn't because she didn't do it any more? Did she try, for another few minutes, to blot out the busy sounds outside and pretend it was Sunday? Did she ask herself if she was at last starting to fall in love with Billy, the patient Northern Irishman who had been courting her for years? 'Bacon and eggs,' she lied.

Miss Vandyk laughed. 'You see what I mean. Nobody ever admits the first thing they think about is sex.'

'Speak for yourself.'

This seemed to please Veronica. 'Well, okay, I will; how kind of you to ask. This morning I woke up in a gorgeous fantasy about a bloke in the Scots Guards, about having it off with him on a horse.'

This was definitely the time to get out of it, but Judy was sniffing the bait: 'On a horse? Galloping?'

'Merde, how painful! No way. Sort of ambling, I guess, much sexier. The only trouble was the horse was so much the nicer. Now — *quel dommage* — I don't know whether to phone him, or the stable. Wotcha think, Mistress Pilgrim?'

Veronica was grinning and Judy, knowing perfectly well that she was opening her stupid mouth wide and closing it on an iron barb, grinned back. 'I'd have the horse.'

'You know, I think you're right. I'm coming to the conclusion that I really don't like men. They chase one so, you see; it's such an effort, so boring, so heavy, so claustrophobic, no space. D'ya think if I wore dirndl skirts with rope sandals and tied a headscarf round my chin they'd lay off so I could do some of the chasing for a change?'

Little bristlings against this bare display of worldly vanity ran up Judy's neck, but she was spared the need to reply because Veronica rattled on. '*Néanmoins*, I ask myself, would one want to chase those charmless apes? Wouldn't one rather chase horses? Wotcha think, Miss Pilgrim?'

Judy, head buried in the filing cabinet, grunted.

'Then, on the other hand, I ask myself, are horses a bit over-endowed for a modest country gal? So would someone who really knew the world, someone like Missy Pilgrim, advise me instead to chase women? Now that would suit me because I like women so much better than men. Yes. Pity they don't turn one on, isn't it?'

Judy, who had now totally forgotten which report she was searching for, hissed, 'Certainly not' and, back at her desk, realized that she was trembling.

She managed to avoid Veronica's corner for the rest of the day by getting a duplicate copy of the missing report from the Department of Trade and Industry. But thoughts about Veronica could not be driven from her mind. What did the woman mean? What was there about Judy that had made her choose to say such vulgar things to her? Was she trying to suggest something about Judy, about herself? What did any of it mean?

The next morning Judy was still thinking about Veronica — not so much thinking as floundering, for her mind was awash with puzzlement. As she showered, noting as she soaped her slender arms, her neat hips, her elegant little toes, her head buzzed helplessly. She dressed in her favourite tartan trousers with the black waistcoat, tied the velvet bow at her throat. She looked nice. She wanted to look nice. Oh vanity, vanity, you foolish Judith Pilgrim, she said to herself, is what comes before a fall.

It was Judy's tea day. (It was always either Judy's tea day or Veronica's as the men were too important to make tea.) As she took Miss Vandyk her steaming mug of sump-oil, she said, as she had prepared herself to say: 'Your coffee,' — pause — 'Veronica.'

Veronica, her long frame folded languidly over the pages of *Playboy* magazine, slowly straightened, slowly lifted the long yellow hair from her eyes, stared straight at Judy, opened her eyes wide and, even more slowly, formed her mouth into a great big sucking kiss.

Judy fled.

Damn. That was twice she'd backed off. Two down against Judy. But she wasn't saying die. No way sister, no way. Her blood was up and she was getting ready for the next round. Meanwhile, if the computer science graduates wanted her help, they could pay for it. So what if she had no qualifications, was a woman, was black, had been in the same grind for ten years: so what. Hers would be the signature at the bottom of the next report on computerization because hers would have been the head that had produced it. If they didn't like her terms, they could do the report themselves.

The computer graduates, perhaps sensing that her blood was up, began to bustle about.

Judy allowed that they were not without initiative. One of them, in his early days at NIPI, had decided to reform the eccentric half-Judy-written program for wool textiles, to bring, he said, a few trillion idle electrons in to bat. As a result, NIPI's system crashed and was out of action till the software specialist came. 'Meeting in Progress' signs appeared on doors and NIPI's corridors exuded fear of a leak to the City. By a miracle, the British economy did not collapse.

However, back to the immediate problem: Veronica's filing was not improving. It was necessary for Judy to spend much of that afternoon searching for the June statistics on woollen tops and yarns. As she went through drawer after drawer, Veronica told her stories about narrow escapes from some persistent bloke in the Household Cavalry who wanted to strip her down so that he could put on her bra. Veronica insisted, passionately, that she always wore bras with acres of lace; she would be more than happy to prove this to Judy if she'd just pop into the loo. Judy declined. She had no problem in believing that, in this at least, Veronica was speaking the truth.

It was only when Judy was back at her desk that she realized that Veronica must deliberately have hidden that report. Why else would it have been found rolled up and stuffed into Judy's umbrella? Veronica didn't know Judy knew, so it was only on a private scoreboard, but Judy sensed with a little thrill some small power over Veronica, and counted it now as one down, and only one to go.

She got that one next day. Veronica asked her to lunch, and Judy had to put her off because she had arranged to meet Billy at John Lewis's to get a lampshade for his mother's birthday. She was a little sorry to realize that this was the first time she had truly found Billy to be an asset.

The barracking continued. Judy accepted that Veronica was not so much patronizing her out of grandness as ragging her out of some real pleasure in bullying; this she minded less. Each morning as she leapt out of bed full of joy at a thought of a day at the office, there got to be less about Veronica that she objected to.

Another day, another misfiled thing. Another search. Work was challenging.

'D'ya like my name, Sunshine?'

'Veronica Vandyk? Sounds a bit like a film star.'

'You don't think it's a real name?'

'No, yes, well — ' Did she? Did she ever believe a word Veronica said? ' — I think it suits you. It's glamorous.'

'Glamorous like a 1930s star though, don't you think. An old woman's name, something out of Agatha Christie or Hitchcock.'

Veronica, who never made the slightest effort to help solve the mystery of the vanishing documents, was combing the fierce little white hairs on her lip with her finger nails, leaving lines on her skin, as if her nail polish had run. There was something so awfully vulnerable about her. Veronica stopped stroking herself.'I was wondering whether I should change it to something more up-to-date, more transatlantic, less county, more, well, *je ne sais quoi.*'

Judy, who understood French perfectly well in France, Guadeloupe, Martinique and back home in Dominica, found Veronica's Franglais rather touching these days, but was not so tender about it that she could pass up the opportunity to get another one up on the scoreboard. 'Jenny Sequin? What a perfect name for you!'

But Veronica had powers of instant recovery. 'More your style, Judy my dear. For myself, I was considering Zoé Zeigler, a touch of your New York, or something really tongue-over-brogues like Sally Pendragon-Smith, or maybe something a bit liberated, like Bette Botte, or Jo Jock, short for jockstrap. But can you think of any nice Chinese names — apart from Susie Wong.'

Judy found herself out of key, half-serious. 'I like Veronica Vandyk best; yes, I like it a lot.'

'Think *ca fait distingué*?'

'Isn't it famous? Is your Daddy a painter or something?'

'Depends on your definition. He tried to paint Mombasa red, and, last time I could be bothered to see him, he was dyeing his face with pink gin.'

This was all Judy needed to conclude that Veronica had had an unhappy childhood and on those grounds to forgive everything from the bottom of her heart.

During this period, NIPI became a wonderful place to be and Judy never said a word to anyone about the misfilings, even though she always had to take the can when deadlines slipped by, even though the other Westindians at NIPI drove her bananas going on about her always being with white people. Nor did she, for some reason, ever tell anything of this to Billy, even when he was pleased that she seemed less tired in the evenings.

Nor, later, was she straight with him about the presents.

The first was on her birthday, a gift right out of the blue, when Judy had already forgotten what day it was. Veronica came over to her desk and shot across its surface a curved yellow stick with a great globe of white bristles on the end, like a giant dandelion. '*Joyeux anniversaire*, darling heart, got you just what every girl needs.'

It was a lavatory brush. The nearest computer science graduate nearly fell off his chair with shock, and kept laughing ages

Miss Vandyk's Game

after Veronica had loped back to her Henry Miller novel. Judy was mortified. Later she noticed the price tag: Veronica had paid £12 for it at Fortnums, a lot of cash to spend on some stupid, perhaps racist, perhaps lesbian, certainly foul, joke. Surely Veronica didn't mean...? Did Veronica think that lavatory brushes were something intimate, perhaps like giving someone silk knickers? Back that evening with Billy she said she'd found it on a bench in the tube.

After that, there were socks with ducks on them that squeaked as you walked, fat white leeks from Berwick Street Market, a water pistol in the shape of a white woman's mouth — gifts always tossed at her casually, to wish her a good weekend, or good luck with her driving test, or to say sorry for breaking Judy's fingernail in the drawer of the filing cabinet. If they hadn't been such queer presents, Judy could have thought she was passing on junk from all those men who chased her so hard.

As it was, she thought — well she didn't know what she thought. Or rather she did. She knew well. She knew in her soul she was cheating on Billy. She knew there was something that hurt her in Veronica's jokes even when she was so possessed by laughter that she feared she might choke. She knew she was playing with fire. She knew she was desperate to discover precisely what she meant to Veronica, and that what she meant had to be a lot. She knew too that when Veronica boasted about being 100 per cent Over The Top that that wasn't all of it: Veronica was a very naughty girl, maybe even a bit of a fruitcake, and dangerous with it. She also knew that Veronica was lonely and unhappy and unloved and beautiful, like a flouncy sad Dominican giant parrot brazening it out in Regent's Park Zoo.

'Hey *pamplemousse*, let's bunk school and go swimming on Hampstead Heath.' Veronica's breath was hot in her ear as Judy (who was more comfortable with maths than with sentences) was struggling with the conclusions of the first report which would carry her signature.

'I haven't got my bathing suit.'

'*Tant pis*. We'll go in the men's pond; there won't be a guard;

there'll be nobody there. Anyway there ought'a be a law against letting someone with such gorgeous tits as you've got squash them into a cozzie.'

'This report — it has to be in tonight.'

'Oh, well — okay then — if you don't want to go.'

'I'm ready.' Judy pushed the papers away.

Veronica was a strong swimmer. Almost as powerful as Judy whose earliest joys were of splashing in any of the hundreds of streams which cascaded out of Dominica's tree-fern forested mountains. Before she was big enough to rate a pair of shoes she would leap far off the basalt rocks, well clear of sea urchins, into the ocean, even on the Atlantic side where the currents might carry you to Bermuda. Dolphin-like, she would swim out to tease the fishermen in their little rocking boats. Here, in the pond, the water was dank and murky and freezing, but Judy was a child again, scooting after the moorhens and charging at the stately Canada geese, splashing her friend's nakedness bright as moonlight, diving between her legs; they were snaking round each other like two slippery fishes.

Veronica's hair had changed to a silky fabric which clung to her shoulders and breasts. As she dipped into the water, Judy watched that thin fabric rise and reveal pink nipples, big and tight against the cold. They were racing. They were chasing. They were teasing. Veronica was giggling, half drowning herself with giggles bubbling up from her navel, giggles telling Judy that Veronica wanted what Judy wanted. And then they were half beached up under the bamboo, where Judy — rocks and roots digging into her shoulder — was kissing skin silky wet, mouthing zigzags down muddy ribs and stomach, and then Judy's brown legs and Veronica's pale legs were tangling in their fight to mash their bodies together.

It didn't have a single thing to do with the report, the awful nervousness Judy felt about going in to NIPI the next morning. Nor did it have anything to do with Billy, who had looked so stricken when she told him she had a thing about somebody else and couldn't go on with him. It had so little to do with Billy that they had both laughed when he confessed, over a reviving cup of tea, that he had his worries too: how could he ever tell his Mother that the nice girl he brought to lunch every other Sunday was a Catholic?

It wasn't Billy; it wasn't work. It wasn't even the moral quandary she was in, though that was serious enough: how could a feeling which all her knowledge told her was wrong make her feel such loving tenderness for all creation? Something at the root of things was uncomfortable and gritty.

She didn't leap out of bed. She let her tea go cold. She took forever to get dressed and was deeply dissatisfied with her neat grey Marks & Spencer trouser suit. 'Vanity, vanity' she said to herself. 'You are guilty of Pride, Judith Pilgrim. You, who don't even know your own heart — and look now how it's caught you out — thought you understood God's plan.' Prophetic words. She stripped off the trouser suit and took out a dress with a Peter Pan collar. Worse. When just about her whole wardrobe was on the bed, and time charging on, she thrust her legs into the tartan trousers and went.

It was Veronica's turn to make the tea that morning. The tray came round. It stopped first at Judy's desk. Judy held her breath, hoping, hoping.

'No sugar for you, *mon ange*: you're quite sweet enough,' Veronica said, and plonked down, on top of the still uncompleted report, a mug not of tea but of sump-oil.

Judy mopped up the spills and pushed the undrinkable stuff away. Her chest was tight with fear. The tray moved on to the desk of the nearest computer science graduate.

Judy didn't look up, but she heard Veronica pinging his braces: 'Gissa thank-you-for-my-cuppa kiss, you great white hope of British industry.'

'Hello, this is an unexpected...'

'*Viens ici* Four-Eyes; even your minimal charms have their moment.'

'Hey, watch it!' His ears would be bright red.

Judy could feel Veronica's excitement rising as the computer graduate struggled helplessly.

'Yes, you hairy pig's belly, let me tell you that I love plain men. The ones you can chase. Me, I chase anything that runs.' She called. 'Judy, sugarplum, come let's you and me pin down this squealing warthog.'

The report was swimming in front of Judy's eyes.

'Oh come on Judy; you're supposed to be a sport.'

Judy's introduction to the report had a plucky little sentence about 'informatics', a subject she barely understood. She would make it a whole damn paragraph! She was out of Miss Vandyk's little game.

Gypsophila

Perhaps I hate gypsophila. It is here in a room lit in part from the leak of light through the door but largely by a great constellation of gypsophila.

In the day there were tiny white flowers threaded with green; tonight only hundreds of points of brightness. They merge here into a Milky Way; there, on the edges, lonely stars are turning.

How strange associations are, things yoked together by one private history. Or even by a non-history, by something that, in Johannesburg's winter more than twenty years ago, didn't happen.

I hadn't even meant to bring her gypsophila. A bottle of wine would have been more appropriate, certainly more useful to me, already stiff with nerves. But although I had thought about the evening all week, nothing practical had presented itself, nothing so sensible as: would I take her champagne, a book, chocolates, flowers (proper flowers, not something that was only just not a weed)?

She hadn't given much of a lead, come to think of it. She had barely described the way to her flat after 'Come and have a bite to eat at my place, say next Wednesday, about eight.' I didn't hear what she was saying at first, there was such a din in the bar, such a din in my head.

It was Johannesburg's only regular gay bar in those days, and not even a proper gay bar. Called The Pro, it was a slit of a place in a drab modern hotel where actors hung out after the theatre. Since the law excluded women from real bars, drinks were poured behind a screen and it rated as a lounge. Since apartheid was a fact of life, only the ponciest of screaming African queens, only the butchest of Indian dykes — non-citizens acceptable so long as they were no more than bedding material — could appear, namelessly. They brought the total numbers to about twenty. Perhaps it wouldn't have been thought of as a gay bar at all had it not been for Beatrice, a huge Boer, well into his fifties. He came in every night at about ten, with carrots in a little wicker basket, to sing dirty songs in a cracked falsetto until closing.

I was also there every night. To feed this habit, I had taken a flat around the corner. I was twenty-one and alone. I had had a lover at school and later languished after various stony-hearted women, but I wasn't looking for a lover, though I thought constantly of love. I was looking, I suppose, for meaning. I was certainly looking.

Sometimes women came in, mostly in twos, and, whatever I was looking for, I would look at them. They had bleached short hair, lacquered into unyielding duck's-arses, masses of lilac or green shadow around eyes ringed with black, no lipstick. They didn't say much to Beatrice or the queens or me, but perched with straight legs on stools, intermittently talking to each other.

Some spoke in English, conversations easy to follow in their confident colonial tones, about who was cheating on whom, what respectable 'BMs' were queers under the blankets, and who had got off with the most gorgeous bird at any of their hundreds of parties.

From other groups I unravelled threads of darker-toned talk, in Afrikaans. Occasionally, these close women would break out to twit Beatrice (fellow-Afrikaner, fellow-pervert, but further down the line) in nervy music-hall English. Sometimes, as they got drunker, voices and fists would rise in fury against the world. Sometimes one or two of them would be loaded into taxis by the management and a wave of relief (or perhaps self-satisfaction) would roll through the bar. There was Evonnie of the powerful musculature who, after a few drinks, would challenge the men to arm-wrestling and lose with very bad grace. Sarie and Sannie would arrive incensed at their boss and leave incensed with each other. Petronella displayed jagged lines on her wrists, carved, she said, with shards of milk bottles.

'We, the Lord's Chosen People,' Beatrice would say; 'we are not couth.' Perhaps for that reason, I was drawn not to the English paper-dolls but these women whose stories were engraved on their faces. Discretion is not an option for Daughters of the Volk guilty of the only unnameable vice of an ethic obsessed with vice. I was also repelled by them, and for the same reason. It was many years and many failures later that I learned not to be shocked by people who wore, ribboned on their chests, their medals of defeat.

Months passed; there were for me no friendships made. In the lavatory sometimes a word was exchanged, but though these were my people, I was not theirs. Their clammed unhappy world would be mine, when I could claim my place. I felt like a child sitting on the edge of a swimming pool, nerving herself against the moment to plunge in.

Then one night the moment chose itself. Diana came in with three dykes—two bleached duck's-arses, one a delicate-featured Indian woman. They all had the same tight trousers and short boots, they sat in the same huddle. But Diana's eyes, great pools of grey, wandered quizzically round the bar, and encountered mine. She held my gaze for a second, then, with a nod, turned back to her friends.

I stared after her and, champion eavesdropper that I was, soon picked up their conversation. Her talk was laced with all the slang I was still learning to push past my lips, but she was not twitting anybody, she was not muttering about what mine magnate's wife was secretly sleeping with what butch, she was complaining in a measured public voice about the working conditions of African actors. She was embarrassing the solitary African there, a pretty young man wearing a coral necklace, perhaps ruining for him a few hours of fantasy, reminding him that the oppressed have a duty to be angry. She wasn't saying anything clever or witty. She had no suggestions about what anyone could do about it. She said nothing that I hadn't heard before. But it brought together all the excitement I had felt at anything said in the bar. I wanted to meet her. I wanted to look through those clear grey eyes that could see our own ghetto with its spider-encrusted wires; see other people's iron ghettos; see beyond.

I didn't have the boldness to break in to her talk (which at her table was being met with yawning indifference). I just sat there and willed her to do something.

She did. She went up to the bar. I emptied my glass at a gulp and followed.

She ordered; I ordered; she half-turned towards me: 'You're not from Johannesburg.'

I nodded.

'Ghastly place.'

I was suddenly shy. Perhaps I grinned.

'You're from?'

'The country. Natal. The Sugar Belt.'

There was a pause. She would soon nod and move off. I had watched too long; my tongue was tangled in my thoughts. I trawled for it. Out gushed, in an awful tweetie-pie voice: 'Sugar cane cutters have even worse working conditions.'

'I'm sure they do.'

Her eyes wandered to my table, took in the plastic handbag and grubby white nylon gloves, then settled beyond, on the Tretchikov print, the one then to be found in every public place and living room, of a rose flung down beside a dustbin. She sighed.

'You shouldn't be drinking brandy and water alone,' she said. 'Come and join us.'

Beatrice, beside us at the bar, had been watching this scene with raised eyebrows, perhaps put out of countenance that Diana had paid no court to him. He seized my hand and pushed a carrot into it. 'Don't do it darling,' he cried, 'You're only a virgin lover once; go for a higher bidder.'

I was startled. I was, to Beatrice, a stranger.

'Thanks Beatrice my angel', Diana took up the challenge, 'We'll call you when the bill's due.'

'You're on, so long as I can watch.' Beatrice bowed as if for an audience, but there was none. Groups at tables were preoccupied with themselves, and Diana was leading me to hers.

I don't remember what she said, what I said, what the dykes said. Only that everything she said was, of course, wise and subtle and funny, that her eyes drank in the world, that in the centre of their grey deepening to black hovered something unfathomable. She was certainly nice to me, inclining her head with great formality to ask if I wanted a cigarette, if I had a job, if I missed my mother, if I lodged nearby, if there were poisonous snakes in the sugar-cane fields. I said yes to all these things.

Then, 'Have a bite at my place,' to which I also said yes.

They pulled on their leather jackets and left before closing time, roaring off on two Lambrettas, one of the dykes with her arms tight around Diana's ribs — into the cold neon-pointed night — Christmas tree gypsophila.

In the seven intervening deserts of nights, she didn't come into the bar. Beatrice's interest in me blossomed. 'Come sit on my knee, girlie,' he would say, 'and hear auntie's warning about the slings and arrows of outrageous fortune. Beware, my lovely, beware of brickies.' The two outsiders now in huddle as exclusive as anybody's, he told me how, in the early hours, he would be haunting the metal halls of the railway station in search of brickies. I don't know if he offered them carrots. He usually found one or two; sometimes he chose badly — or perhaps too accurately — and ended up in hospital. He occasionally picked up a policeman by mistake, the other difference being that then he'd have to call the ambulance himself. 'Let auntie's ruined complexion,' he would say, 'be a lesson to you of the perils of crawling outside the laager,' and his crumpled face, brandy-scented grease oozing from its open pores, would bear down on mine. 'You, little girl, you still have a choice. Let Mama pick you a husband and buckle down to it. Do as auntie says and you'll get a garden with a swimming pool in it. You can spend your days there, dreaming about lesbian ladies over your G&T.'

And again: 'Mama must make it one of those men who grows fat when he gives up rugby; an army chappie say, thick as two short planks, a bloke who talks in grunts. He won't pry into your soul; he won't notice if you do your nails while he's screwing you.'

Beatrice's two great hands, nails earthstained as hooves, would cradle mine. Sometimes he tutted over my nails, bitten to the quick. 'Oh poor little claws. Why do women destroy their few weapons? Sharpen them, my angel, like a cat. Then you can teach your soldier to be a good boy. But first Mama must choose right. Tell her auntie Beatrice will advise.'

The thought of Beatrice and my mother talking, even being in the same room, was so shocking that I laughed hard for minutes.

Beatrice, who had so recently seemed repulsive to me, whom I had feared because I could never tell when he was sending me up, became, in those seven nights, my best friend. He poured his accumulated despair into my ears. He came to my flat, and we slept in the one bed, chaste as nuns: I was clearly not much cop as a brickie. We bumped across town to his smallholding, to see neat rows of winter vegetables and the filthy shack in which he cooked and occasionally washed, and bedded his brickies. We drank a lot of brandy together, and I found the sensation of workdays wobbly with hangover disturbingly pleasurable: they distanced me from the granite edifice of work. I grew able to treat the heap of papers on my desk with indifference. Faces at work which used to burn into my consciousness faded to ashes. I didn't eat much, though I had an endless supply of carrots, but got through a pack and a half of untipped Lucky Strike every day. And the dark and dangerous world he sketched and which I now found myself entering became increasingly fascinating. If I had read Genet, I would have been able to define this excitement. Definitionless, I poured all those feelings into the image of a woman with quizzical grey eyes.

I devoured every scrap of information about Diana. She came from Cape Town. She believed in God and tore strips off people who mocked her for it. She was a theatre set designer. The three women with her were freelances, employed by her for one production, a musical based on a story by Alan Paton. She read thrillers. Her lover had gone off to Nyasaland with a liquor-shop owner. She designed her shirts and had them made up by an Indian tailor. She lived alone in Doringbos, an area freshly whitened by the Group Areas Act. It was now largely occupied by white railway workers, the State having given them first option to buy there, to beat down the prices asked by the evicted coloured families. Beatrice didn't much like Diana. 'She's cold, sweetheart, and a snob, like all cold women.'

All this, even the horrible place she lived, increased her glamour. That her one mind could command so easily the world of The Pro (which was to me the gay world) and the granite edifice beyond seemed miraculous. She had asked me to dinner. She could unseal the doors of a mind. Well before that Wednesday dawned, I was obsessed.

Beatrice, enticingly discouraging, bid me a lugubrious farewell on Tuesday night. He warned me that Diana tended to go on about things; if she did, I was to launch into song with 'You ain't nothing but a hound dog', since Diana loathed pop music. He was sure Diana wasn't the sort who would ask vulgar questions about butch or femme, but if the subject came up, I was to say that I was absolutely brilliant at both. Then he advised Listerine for the breath and silk knickers for the arse and gave me a bunch of carrots to take as an offering.

I didn't take the hint. Wednesday was so crammed with deciding what socks, what opening remarks (and how to get from them to an exploration of psyches), what to do if she fed me soft eggs or bloody steak (things that turn my stomach over), that I didn't think of Beatrice's carrots rotting in the sink. I didn't question, either, what I knew I wanted to do: to go to Doringbos on foot — not a great distance, in fact, but absolutely not to be done in a city where every night the streets were emptied of citizens by the pass laws.

It was only when I set out across the tsotsi-infested streets of Hillbrow — nerving myself to pass from there through the unlit pool of Berea to Doringbos where there might still be children playing rounders among the parked cars — that it came to me. I had no offering. Between a beerhall and a filling station huddled a little flower shop, its frontage a mist of gypsophila. The night was cold, and the wet streaks that ran from the flower buckets to the gutter glistened with the threat of ice. The smell of vegetation mingled with hops and petrol. I would bring to Diana that musky greenness, armfuls of flowers over which her eyes could wander. Inside, there were roses, red, pink and yellow; there were bold, theatrical strelitzias; yard-long gladioli and canna lilies; there were grey and purple proteas — rolled-up hedgehogs, the national flower. Outside, in the cold, gypsophila stars trembled.

I went in. 'How much is the gypsophila?'

His voice was tense: 'The baby's-breath? This stuff? This was left over from a First Communion at that Roman place up the road. Hell Dametjie, I wouldn't lie to you: it was a First Communion for a bunch of kaffirs. Really, man, all dressed up in white, carrying prayer books and candles!'

Oh, my countrymen. Depression familiar as sin clouded the pretty little shop.

'You don't want them, no? Well, they have been aired. Say 20 cents a bunch.'

Not possible; they were too cheap.

He misread my hesitation. 'Ag man, just take the lot.'

No need to panic. No need to run. The shop was no more awful than the rest of the world. I looked round for alternatives. Roses — too intimate; strelitzias — ugly; gladioli — common; what? I picked up a protea, two, three. Perhaps they were all right. No scent, no velvet texture, no glow, but they were handsome. And she came from the Cape. And they were suitably expensive. They would do. On the way out, I paused again at the gypsophila. Why not? I took as much as I could carry, and made up an unlikely bouquet of delicate white points with the three woody desert heads in the centre.

No inconspicuous passage through Berea was now possible; I was lit by a candelabrum of gypsophila. One kerb-crawler I escaped by dropping into the vestibule of some flats; another followed for several blocks, leaning out of his window to whistle, but fortunately not getting out of his car. The third didn't proposition but drove behind at walking pace, hissing insults about low white women. He seemed to be on his way to Doringbos. Perhaps his daughters were just then playing rounders in the street. I walked fast, stopping only to answer the greeting of two black streetboys strumming a guitar made from a paraffin can. They admired the flowers. They were protection for a few minutes, and they didn't find it odd that there should be a lone white woman on the street after dark. I gave them a few cents which they rolled up in tattered handkerchiefs and stuffed into their shorts. Perhaps that night, if the police didn't pick them up, they would sleep curled round central heating vents.

In Doringbos, there were smells of frying boerewors and the yells of children fighting inside the carcasses of wrecked cars. I found Diana's place, a tall, dark house with sash windows, pressed against the cliff which separated Doringbos from Highlands. Years later, I saw houses like that in Muswell Hill, and found them as forbidding even though they were on top of the cliff.

I checked my watch. Arrived early, and safe. I shouldn't have walked of course. I should have confessed that I had no car and asked Diana to pick me up. Would I ask her to drive me back? Would I have to go back? Perhaps we would talk long into the night about this city, about this country, and perhaps she would say it could be saved. But perhaps she would be irritated that I had been silly enough to walk, perhaps she would want to lecture me and tie me down to the granite edifice. If she did, could I say that one tried to make something right by acting as if it were? To Beatrice, to whom nothing and everything was ludicrous, I could have said that I wanted to strip down, come dressed only in my soul. Could I approximate, say to Diana that I had wanted to do something dangerous, endure some foolish ordeal, because perhaps there was nothing that was real that was not plucked from the jaws of a shark? If I had known it, perhaps I could have said that like our mother Eve, like all her daughters, I was seeking knowledge of good and evil. Not the dessicated wisdom of the Catechism but of the living tree, living serpent. Or that I, like so many of Eve's daughters, like Eve herself who had lured her baby-faced Adam into the adventure, lacked courage to pluck the apple alone and wanted Diana to lead me by the hand. Safest to let her think I had taken a taxi.

The gypsophila bundle half behind my back, I rang the bell. After a long time, the peephole darkened, and the door opened on a coloured woman hauling on a dressing gown.

'You're for Diana?' She had recognized me as a lesbian as quickly as I had recognized her as black and therefore living in the house illegally. Diana would have collaborated in this. The woman had taken a risk in opening the door.

I ventured a smile. 'Good evening.'

'The flat round the back.' She gestured.

'Thank you very much. Thank you very... .' The door had shut.

With a light heart, I trotted round past the dustbins, stopping to note the reflection of the big African moon from the gypsophila. The coloured woman didn't look like a theatre person; she was tight-lipped, even arrogant; could she be a member of *Umkhonto we Siswe** in hiding? Might I, who could walk the streets of Johannesburg at night, become a runner for them? Would this be one of the things Diana would initiate me into? Even in winter, when it doesn't rain for months, the place, overhung as it was by the cliff, smelled damp, vegetable, tumescent with new life. I felt my way for the last few steps, till helped by a light from somewhere inside. The door was open.

'Hello.' I carried the flowers high before me. 'Hello, hello, Diana.' A white-painted hall, a living room crammed with books and one of those new tape recorders, a glimpse of a neat bedroom with a Basuto blanket serving as counterpane. A beautiful place in the midst of all that awfulness. 'Diana?'

In the kitchen, an African maid was ironing shirts. 'The Missus is working,' she said in a tired voice. 'It's the dress rehearsal tomorrow.'

'She's expecting me.'

'You want to wait?'

I did. I sat on soft chairs and hard chairs. I explored the flat. I looked at my watch. I walked to the road. The curtains were drawn upstairs. The children had gone. I walked back. I searched the shelves in vain for banned books. I looked at my watch again.

---

* *Umkhonto we Siswe: Spear of the Nation; the military wing of the African National Congress*

It hadn't stopped. I examined the tape recorder but didn't dare to try it. I walked back to the road again. I listened to the iron bumping. I tried not to think it peculiar that a revolutionary should have a maid who called her 'Missus'. I helped myself to a glass of water. I failed to get a conversation going with the maid.

At nine she said she was going and wanted to lock up. 'That's okay.' I said. I put the flowers in the butler's sink, fluffing out the gypsophila. 'Goodnight,' I said, and went.

Her keys jangled. How did she get home, or did she, too, squat illegally on the premises? I walked, itching to put my fist through the gob of every kerb crawler.

But I didn't go home. I went to The Pro. I went up and put my arms round Beatrice. 'Oh, you appalling creature,' he cried, 'What on earth are you doing here? You've just ruined my best fantasy this week. It was taking cream-cakes to you and Diana in bed.' I had my face flat against Beatrice's carrot-juice stained shirt and was sobbing.

'Oh sweetheart,' he said, dropping cigarette ash in my hair, 'if you only knew how much I love women who can still cry. Now I'm crying too, and it's utterly delicious. In my next life, I'll ask them to make me a lesbian.' I don't know how I got home. I was certainly very drunk.

I didn't go to the bar the next evening. If I was too sick to go to work, I was too sick for that. I cleaned the flat. There was no way out. Diana had forgotten. My odyssey was a very small show when there were dress rehearsals. I looked at myself in the mirror and saw one of twenty million bodies bred in a poisoned soil. If I could be allowed no inner life, perhaps at least I could pledge this body to freedom, fight and follow the leaders — Mandela, Sisulu, Mbeki, Goldberg — follow them to prison. I had lived two decades and done nothing to change the ugliness. I hadn't even thought about it except as a reflection of my own discontent. Perhaps the revolution would not be too proud to accept a lesbian. I looked at my mirror image again: I had thought Diana might have liked that little triangle of dark hair. I ran my fingers through it, and it sprang back into curls, so gutsy, even on me, someone with head hair as straight and lifeless as nylon thread. I stared into the mirror and tears welled up in pity for a vain and idle daydreamer who so craved to be part of something great.

The door bell rang. The peephole showed Diana. I scrubbed my face and ran for some clothes.

'Beatrice sent me.' She came in grumpily. 'Why did you rush off like that last night? Couldn't you wait a few minutes? There was a lot of traffic.' She stood with her hands in her pockets. Her eyes were fixed on the blackened window. She did not incline her head, elegantly, as she spoke. Her leather jacket was buttoned tight across her chest.

We were on her Lambretta charging through Hillbrow, Berea; we flashed past the two streetboys; we swung round the cliff to Doringbos. We were parked half inside the hedge with the saddlebags locked against the attentions of children. We felt our way round to the back. She was banging pans in the kitchen, throwing together a meal. It was probable that I would sleep that night under the Basuto blanket.

She kept breaking off to answer the phone: people wanting changes made to the backdrop, a door to hang the other way, different lighting at the end of the overture. Nothing about *Umkhonto*.

I didn't take any phone messages; I didn't lift pans starting to burn in the kitchen. I was feeling the rugged sepals of the proteas, thrust into in a thick brown earthenware jug. They hadn't opened any further, but then they unravel very slowly. Proteas last for weeks — for ever, if you like dried flowers. There was no sign of the gypsophila.

Perhaps the seeds of this brilliant constellation were scattered in the same Big Bang that made that other, older galaxy I thought, as I stood in the doorway of a room in London, looking at gypsophila, more than twenty years later.

Many things have scattered. London jostles with exiles, among them Diana, among them me. I hope the young man with the coral necklace escaped, but I fear he did not. Beatrice didn't escape; nor, I suppose, did the Afrikaans dykes. Perhaps they still drink at a descendant of The Pro, whispering fearfully of what will follow the brutal and now doomed order which gave them, and me, a gangster protection. They were not on an ascending curve: perhaps they live with ferocious dogs behind high walls; perhaps they are old and ill, or mad; perhaps they are dead.

Certainly many things have died. But there is still the Roman Church where gypsophila flowered at First Communion ceremonies. The white people have abandoned it for their exclusive chapels in the suburbs and all the prayer books there are held in black hands. Would Diana remember that church? Would she remember if I asked her what became of that other First Communion gypsophila, if she gave it to the maid?

Sparrow

Pattie peered into the staffroom. 'The only way to get any maths through their skulls,' someone was saying, 'is to rub it against their ears.' So far, so good; he was not talking about her. She went in. She greeted nobody. She walked all the way round to the teapot. Eugenie, now screened by heads, did not look up.

A few seconds later, Pattie, mug in hand, was out in the coolness, heading towards the science hut. For what it was worth, the foray back to the staffroom could be judged an achievement. Perhaps they were too short of science teachers to sack her. Anyway, Cleo might be kind to her tomorrow. Anyway, anyway, so long as suicide existed, you could always have the last word.

Pattie had not picked out Eugenie for a friend. On her first day at Neasden Middle, London, she had thought all the staff a bunch of lumps apart from the Australian supply teacher, long since gone back to her land of sunshine. It was the Number 16 bus which brought the two young women together; that, and Pattie's never having an umbrella.

Not that Eugenie was a lump. She did live with her aunt, but that was excusable since she couldn't have got a room with floorboards strong enough to take a piano on what they paid probationary music teachers. As far as looks went, she was the opposite of a lump. A bit too ready-made perhaps, with a high colour and one of those chiseled faces that look even better in middle age; a handsome, tidy, Jewish-looking girl who would always be the team captain; a 1950s girl in 1970; someone who dared to say that Pinter was boring and had never heard of Janis Joplin.

But Pattie and Eugenie were both questing: not for each other, certainly; nor for the same thing. And they were both new to London, both twenty-one, and neighbours. So a friendship rooted itself, which was strong enough, though at first perhaps neither regarded it as important. Eugenie seemed to like having Pattie around to talk to about her boyfriends and Pattie was glad to escape from hers. Eugenie took Pattie shopping for clothes, and Pattie, dressed in Eugenie's decisions, did indeed feel more confident and feminine. Miss Currie seated them together in the staffroom and Eugenie's Auntie Brenda made sure that Pattie sometimes ate greens. Things rolled easily through the autumn and winter term.

Then Eugenie found what she had been looking for. Ralph, Neasden's own prodigy, who had made it into the back row of fiddles in the London Symphony Orchestra, was assigned one afternoon a week with the music classes. He had floppy hair and the longest fingers possible, and talked wittily about queers in the music world. All the girls immediately fell in love with him, and so did Eugenie. She played some Chopin duets with him, and found that she had never played so well. He was very kind and said she showed promise. They stayed on after school to practice some more, and Ralph took her home in his Alpha Romeo. Eugenie was ecstatic on the bus the next morning, and Pattie felt a twinge of pain, though she was pleased for her friend.

Then one Friday Ralph gave Eugenie a ticket to his concert, and Eugenie asked for two, so that Pattie could come as well. And she wanted Pattie to be allowed backstage afterwards. Pattie accepted, aware that if the tables had been turned, she might not have been as generous. So, wearing low-cut dresses selected by Eugenie, they took the tube to the West End.

Pattie, who had never been to a real concert before, was overwhelmed by the grandeur of it all. Ralph looked very distinguished: Pattie agreed that he was definitely the handsomest man in the orchestra, but wasn't entirely sure about the flautist Eugenie picked out for her. She wondered what Eugenie, or anybody, would think if they knew that her attention was absorbed by a cellist, a sharp-chinned little woman with tired eyes. The cellist had gone when they met Ralph backstage, but the flute man was friendly.

They became a threesome, sometimes, with the flautist, a foursome. Eugenie liked the arrangement and Ralph never seemed to mind one way or another, but Pattie felt discontented and frumpish.

That was the mood she was in when Ralph announced that he had planned something very special for Pattie that evening. None of Eugenie's wiles could drag out of him any more than that it was a club in Chelsea, and Pattie would meet some of his special friends. But it had to be important; Ralph was excited: his normally pale face was flushed and he gave off a sweetish, medicinal smell — not his aftershave, Pattie suspected, but drink. Unpleasant. Eugenie dressed Pattie in a pink silk shirt-waister, her hair in a ponytail — what did it matter to Pattie if it made her look about thirteen? And what did it matter if, when Ralph said they'd need a splash of Dutch courage and brought out a bottle of whisky to drink in the car, she topped hers up with Coke. She drank it didn't she? More than you could say for Eugenie who had asked for it neat.

The place was an absolute slum; Pattie's heels sank into the decayed linoleum of a staircase down to a basement smelling of beer and dry rot. The noise was painful. A ferocious-looking woman at the door greeted Ralph with a kiss like a dogbite and motioned them into a corner.

'Sorry chaps,' Ralph said. 'In spite of a healthy reputation, I'm just baggage here until Cleo claims us. Patience my souls. She'll be along.'

As Pattie's eyes got used to the darkness, they widened in surprise: the place, which at first had seemed like one of those drinking clubs in Manchester you saw in films, was jammed with women, laughing, squawking, dancing with each other. She looked at Eugenie, tense under the camellia pinned to her chest. Eugenie had once talked about strange things in Paris a long time ago, where, in salons dripping with gold leaf and lilies, women poets in monocles conducted secret liaisons with the daughters of defunct royal houses. Pattie had been embarrassed at that telling and cut Eugenie short. She wanted to know more, but not from Eugenie. This place was certainly not Paris. These women were loud and loutish, prancing about like Neasden Middle when the bell rang. For all that, Pattie peered closely at the faces, in case there might somewhere be just one....

Then, bursting through the throng of dancers, came on long strides a figure six feet tall and lean as an arrow.

'Ah, Ralphie my darling!' Arms reached out towards him and there emerged the most extraordinary creature Pattie had ever seen: her whole manic frame in black; her mass of hair red as blood against a dead-white face tinged with grey veins; her eyes riverwater in a valley of magenta eye shadow; deep grooves beside her mouth doubling its great width. 'Oh Lord,' said Eugenie, grasping Pattie's arm, 'Medusa advancing on us.'

Several inches taller than Ralph, the woman wrapped him in snaky arms. Eugenie stiffened. Pattie could smell a musky perfume.

'This, Cleo my angel,' said Ralph, 'is my girlfriend Eugenie.' Eugenie nodded.

'And this is my girlfriend's girlfriend Pattie, someone I'd particularly like you to meet.' Eugenie's fingers tightened round Pattie's elbow.

'Pattie, how nice, how sweet; you're like a little bird.' — Pattie curled her lips in something she believed resembled a snarl — 'Can you sing?'

'Not yet,' offered Ralph, 'but perhaps you could teach her.'

'Are you a musician too?' came from Eugenie, to hoots of laughter from Ralph.

'No my dear, too long in the cage,' the woman said, in that voice like a someone in the theatre, yet not unkindly.

Cleo went off to get them a bottle of wine (men, being baggage, were not allowed at the bar), and swept a table clear for them to sit at. Women, thumping and sweating, pounded by, taking no notice.

Conversation was difficult in the din. Pattie sat with Eugenie's fingers still encircling her elbow, her head spinning with nervousness and some strange excitement. If only Eugenie would go away, give her a chance to think, to get some measure of that rather awful woman, find out how Ralph knew that these rather awful people had anything to do with her. Eugenie was plying him with questions. Pattie leaned over to listen.

'Cleo,' he was saying, 'is a great friend of Sergei ---- ' (he imitated somebody wielding a conductor's baton and then put a finger significantly to his lips) 'and Sergei is also rather fond of me. Get it?' Pattie looked at Ralph, grinning to himself, and nodded. She didn't get it at all. Perhaps Eugenie, who was looking murderous, did.

Sergei's lanky friend dumped two bottles of wine on the table. 'Use those old beerglasses there,' she said. 'That's right, just rinse them out with a little wine. Tip the lees on the floor.' She demonstrated, then filled the half-pint glass almost to the brim, and handed it to Pattie. 'So, my dear, is this your first taste of London life?'

Pattie felt shy. 'Sort of,' she said, regretting the pink dress and pony tail.

'Is this what you came to find, little sparrow?'

Pattie made an effort. 'Actually, my name is Patricia.' And then, with another effort, 'Yes, it is what I came to find. I think it's what I came to find.'

'And do you like what you see?'

'It isn't like I expected.'

'Things in the hand are always a little disappointing,' said Cleo, a smile gentling her huge mouth. 'They look best in the shop window, don't they?'

Pattie looked up into great tiger's eyes blazing right on her. Her insides turned to water. She started back, then grasped the beer glass, aware of the wine jumping up and down as she brought it to her lips.

Cleo pulled a large linen handkerchief out of her pocket. 'You spilled your wine,' she said, leaning forward and carefully wiping Pattie's chin.

Pattie took a great hold of her courage. 'The glass was too full.'

Then, with another struggle: 'I've only looked through the shop window before, but now I want to go in.'

'Indeed? I hope it goes very well for you.' Cleo rose on her long legs. 'Well, good luck then, sparrow.'

'Oh, you aren't going yet?' Pattie put in hastily.

The big eyes were vague. 'Oh well; okay then. I suppose we mustn't disappoint Ralph. Want to dance?'

Pattie hadn't danced with a woman since she was at school. She wasn't quite sure what to do. She stood up on wobbly legs. But when she was wrapped in the long arms and swept off into the throng, it seemed like flying. Despite her partner's tall boots and her wretched stilettos, they moved very easily, her legs taking up the rhythm of the long hard legs, her hand tentative on a snake-like long back; and, when the music and crowd pressed them closer, came the strange thrilling sensation of touching her cheek against a cheek that had not been roughened by a razor. The hard edges of two forearms slid against her ribs, pressing them, 'This what you're looking for, little bird?'

'Yes.'

'There's plenty of it about.'

When the music came to an end, and Cleo bowed low then turned away, Pattie made her way thoughtfully to the table. She flushed to see Eugenie's eyes and mouth round as little pebbles.

'Think you made a hit there Pattie.' Ralph was rubbing his hands together, 'Eh, a little bird, are we? We like old Cleo Cadaverous do we? Think I've got the Third Eye, do we?'

'Ralph you're drunk and horrible,' Eugenie hissed. 'Leave Pattie alone. She's my friend.' Then, *sotto voce* to Pattie, 'Don't dance with her again. Say No. That's what I'll do, for sure. She's weird. We might catch something.'

Cleo, towering above the crowd, was dancing with someone else. Someone properly dressed in flared jeans. Pattie tried not to mind their intertwined arms, tried not to care that Cleo was so extraordinary, so mysterious, so glamorous that every one of those women must be watching her. Now Cleo was at the bar, pressing her long ribs against it, reaching, pulling the lobe of the barmaid's ear. Then she was out of sight. Pattie's eyes raked the club till they found her, slouched against a back wall, a long black cigarette holder dangling out of her mouth.

'You're staring at that freak, Pattie,' said Eugenie in a miserable voice.

'Yes,' said Pattie. 'I don't care; I'm going to ask her to dance.' Which she did. And again. And again. Each time, Cleo said 'Okay sparrow,' but didn't detain her after. Sitting out the next one, barely conscious of Ralph's high amusement or of Eugenie fretting to go home, she still couldn't take her eyes off Cleo. Soon she was off again, in pursuit.

Once more Cleo's forearms tightened against her sides. 'You've been making sheep's eyes at me all evening, little sparrow,' she said. 'I think you're upsetting your friend.'

'Too bad.'

'Shouldn't you stay with her awhile?'

'Why?'

'Perhaps she cares for you, and that don't come cheap.'

'I want to stay with you.'

'You want to go someplace with me?'

'Yes.'

Cleo sighed. 'What a little bossyboots you are.'

Pattie lost the sense of gravity in a huge bedroom, heavy with Cleo's perfume, that, except for the slippery white sheets under her, seemed wholly clad in white angora. She was somewhere in, perhaps, St John's Wood, in the lair of the extraordinary creature that had led her in and then, standing tall as the Archangel Michael in all that whiteness, had left her saying, 'Wait here, little lamb.'

All was not quite well. Cleo had been gone too long. Had Pattie done something to show how green and ignorant she was? Had Cleo just lost interest? Or was this when she was supposed to be undressing, getting out of this stupid pink thing? Should she wash? She undid her hair, and it fell sweetly to her shoulders. She hoped Cleo would like its softness against her own fierce red mane. A beautiful warrior's mane. She thought of a shoulderblade, a thigh, a voice. She would lose her mind if she thought of the eyes.

It was getting to be a very long time. Why was everything so quiet? Why no traffic, no radios? Where was the rattling of window panes as buses passed? Why hadn't Cleo kissed her? 'Cleo,' she called timidly. Silence. She fingered the elaborate curls of the bedhead, the brass clean and cold to the touch. Where was this place? That was a panelled white door with gold knob, leading to a bathroom, also white and gold. Those french doors behind the white velvet curtains opened to a balcony and dark glimpse of Regents Park treetops. That was Pattie's handbag, that plastic lump on the white leather pouffe, with money in it for a taxi. Those were her stilettos, those things like dogturds in the snowy carpet. That? A cupboard? She opened. Inside, in the oiled mahogany void, on little hooks neat as a row of executions, hung ropes, chains, thongs, handcuffs. She banged it shut. Had she screamed? Why was she shaking? Run, where to run? Her stilettos? She shrank from them; couldn't bear to cripple her feet in their steel and leather.

Her fumbling fingers found a door, with far beyond, a light. She crept closer, saw the back of a big armchair, and the hair flaming in a pool of lamplight.

'Cleo,' she called, running up to her.

Very slowly the head lifted, the eyes huge and almost transparent, unfocused. Cleo seemed to have begun to undress; she was still wearing the boots and black dress-shirt, but her trousers were tossed on the floor and long thighs emerged from lacy black silk.

Cleo's arms reached out. 'It's you, my innocence. Come sit by me. I'm having second thoughts.' Her voice was husky, slow, breaking, as if she had bubbles in her throat.

Pattie crawled into her arms and Cleo began to fondle her hair absently. In a low tone: 'Do you want anything, baby? Do you use anything? I've got most things.'

'I want *you*,' Pattie answered fiercely, and began to kiss wrists, neck, needle-sharp bones of a shoulder.

'Can you imagine, little sparrow, how many times I've played this little piece of theatre with how many pretty girls?'

'A dozen, a million. I don't care.'

'Or ever know how cold my heart is?'

'I'll warm it.'

'You will?' That strange smile flickered. 'That's nice. But your friend, she'll turn against you, you know; you'll be shaming her.'

'She can do what she likes. Oh Cleo, please, don't get onto that. Here: Cleo, want me.' Fumbling in hurry, she unbuttoned the shirt, and pressed her lips into deep hollows under collarbones, then throat, then against wonderfully delicate breasts that barely rose from the bone. 'Cleo, you're so beautiful,' she whispered. 'Cleo, I've fallen terribly in love with you. Why won't you kiss me?'

'Don't be a fool.' Cleo pushed her away. 'You're turned on because you're tasting your first freedom; it's yourself you're excited about.' Cleo's eyes became vague again. 'You don't know me, baby. You don't know how I live. You don't know what I do, do you? You don't even know my name. I've forgotten yours, you know.'

She flushed. 'It's Patricia Monica Symons.'

'Your real name?'

'Of course its my real name.'

'The kitten has claws. That's nice. That's really quite nice. What a shame. Well, you've called the suit. So you fancy me, do you sparrow?'

'More than anything.'

'Madly? With every bone, every nerve?'

'Every single one.'

'But I scare you, yes?'

Pattie grinned. 'Yes, actually, you do a bit.'

'Oh shit! I wish you weren't such a nice kid. Well, have it your way then, but don't say I didn't try.'

The eyes, suddenly hard, wandered over Pattie's breasts and stomach. Then, coldly, came a: 'Get up.' Cleo motioned Pattie out of the chair and stood her between her knees. 'You want this?' Pattie nodded. 'Sure?'

'Sure.'

'All right; take off your clothes. Yes, all of them. I need to look at you. No, not round the back of the chair. Here. That's better. Roll the tights up nicely.' Cleo lay back, arms behind her head, legs spread long and wide. 'Now go to the window and walk back towards me. Slow. Don't grin like that. It makes you look nervous.'

When Cleo slowly rose on legs that were marble white and too thin and the most beautiful Pattie had ever seen, and slowly pressed hands like a vice into the sides of Pattie's pelvis, Pattie realized that she was shaking all over.

'Like holding a little wild bird,' muttered Cleo, the huge pupils of her eyes flooding Pattie's. 'But now I've got to screw you.'

Bus rattling the window pane, and morning crashed in on Pattie like the Falling Tower. Cleo — oh my God! The sun on the dogeared science workbooks, on the fablon-coated table with Baby Belling and coffee mugs, in a pool on the worn carpet, was awful, accusing. She turned her face away. What terrible thing had she done? What act of arson had she committed, setting a torch to her own life? How was her body still here, and breathing? She lifted the blankets — white belly, white thighs — and closed them down with disgust.

Cleo — oh my God! No she couldn't call on God. Cleo? Cleo was a tiger. Pattie had known she was a tiger. Pattie had made her into a tiger. Why? What was there in Pattie to call up such things? Why wouldn't Cleo kiss her? Then the tiger was on her and wouldn't stop, and all the while Pattie couldn't get out of her mind the horrible things strangling in the cupboard. And those cries that broke out of Cleo, like someone was killing a pig. But it was she, Pattie, who was the pig. Poor pigs, that never did any harm to humans, yet they cram them in filthy pens all their lives then chop them up and say Grace over the pieces. Tears of pity for pigs rushed into Pattie's eyes. Poor destroyed pigs. Poor Pattie.

Poor Pattie alone. For when Cleo was through with it all and Pattie whimpering, Cleo had pushed her, more or less dressed again, into a taxi and thrust into her hand a ten-pound note for the fare. The fare, seven shillings, Pattie had paid out of her own money. She'd flushed the note down the lavatory. But Cleo's card was still, crumpled, in her hand. In an elaborate script on deckled green parchment it read 'Cleo — masseuse — REG 4783'. Pattie buried her head in the pillows and let the sobs shake her body to pieces.

She spent the rest of the day in Fortune Green Cemetery, somewhere Eugenie would never find her. Pattie could never be the same again. Something in her had been slaughtered. These people visiting their civilized dead were not more grieved than she, but her grief alone was foul and shameful. Cleo was right. Pattie had betrayed Eugenie, the one person in this merciless city who cared for her, and she would never be able to face her again. By evening, her body was wracked with a hateful sick longing for Cleo which made her want to scream.

Monday she skipped school. Tuesday she had to go in because the bunsen burners were to be serviced. She walked the three miles to Neasden to avoid the Number 16 bus, trying to will herself back to life, to stop weeping over pigs, to stop this dragging wanting all the time, to stop being so frightened and miserable. She went direct to the science hut.

It was at first break, when she was dusting iron filings off the magnets, that she heard Eugenie's footstep. It was a calm, even footstep. She felt Eugenie's hand on her shoulder. It was gentle. She fought a rush of new tears.

'Oh Pattie, that woman; she was so repulsive — like a witch — like a vampire. It was awful to see you... . I can't bear anything to hurt you. I'm going to kill Ralph for this.'

Pattie flung herself into Eugenie's warm, strong arms and sobbed until the bell rang.

Pattie took up knitting, using Eugenie's favourite patterns. Eugenie spent a lot of time with her, bringing her flowers, little cakes she had baked. She often held her in her arms and rocked her. She wanted Pattie to move in to Auntie Brenda's place so that she could calm her in the night against her nightmares. And she was understanding when Pattie said No, though Pattie didn't explain why — that she couldn't bear Eugenie to see her filthy body. Eugenie just took her hand and swore that Pattie would be her best friend for ever. When they married, Eugenie said, they would live next door to each other and treat each other's children as their own.

Pattie never knew what Eugenie said to Ralph about Cleo, because the subject was never mentioned, although Ralph was flirty with Pattie in a way that made her feel worse. Eugenie said she would marry Ralph if that was all right with Pattie, but before that was settled Pattie should get fixed up so that they could have a double wedding. Ralph's Alpha took them to the zoo, East Lane Market, lots and lots of concerts.

Often, the flautist was there too, wearing grey flannel trousers and brown shoes. The boys chaffed each other a lot, and, watching them, Pattie knew it was getting to be time she went to bed with the flautist. Burdened with a great pain in her chest, Pattie felt older, more tolerant. He was a little shy with her alone. She wanted to make it easier for him.

But all the while, every waking or sleeping second, it was running through her mind that one day, perhaps that very day, Cleo would be found dead, from an overdose, malnutrition, perhaps murder. Or she would die of an endless stream of pretty girls and nobody to love her.

These thoughts rolled round her head that Friday as she and Eugenie washed their hands after doing dinner duty, and went to spend the precious last few minutes of the lunch break in the sun, planning the weekend's picnic on Hampstead Heath.

Eugenie had the list. 'Sausage rolls. Cucumber sandwiches on brown. Chilled Frascati and four glasses. Napkins. Chicken legs. A really crisp green salad. Enough vegetarian stuff there for you, Pattie, or shall we add some cottage cheese? Yes, cheese puffs. Now, clothes.' Eugenie thought. 'The forecast is for gorgeous weather, so let's take our big straw hats. I'm doing a new ribbon for yours.' She looked sideways at Pattie. 'You look so smashing in that straw hat. It dapples your shoulders. You've got super shoulders, dainty bones; not like me. Yet you tan so nicely, its a shame to wear a hat. Hat, no hat: I don't know which would be better. Decisions! Oh decisions!'

Cleo, so pale, would always have to wear a hat. Pattie had

never seen her in the sun. That bedroom would look fungus-yellow in sunlight. Perhaps Cleo hated the sun — perhaps she hated day.

An image of lamplight falling on long white legs and a black dress-shirt rose in front of her. She looked up into eyes like riverwater. Oh, Cleo, why couldn't it have been different? Oh, why hadn't she...? Why couldn't she...? Why didn't she...? Why not, when it was the only thing. She would seize her courage. Now.

'Excuse me a minute, Genie,' she snapped. She was up and running to the phone in the secretary's office. Her fingers had dialled the number before she'd paused to get out of her purse a worn parchment card.

'Hello?' drawled the voice, sending tinglings down Pattie's arms and legs.

'Cleo?'

'Oh?' — there was a pause — 'Well, if it isn't the little sparrow.'

'You remember?'

'After a fashion, babe. You've just woken me up.'

'Cleo. Can I see you again?'

'A-ha' — another pause — 'I wasn't planning on it. I'm a bit taken up with one thing and another.'

Damn. Pattie was trembling again. But this was a different kind of trembling. This time she knew what she was doing. The sun poured in through the window and in a minute the bell would shatter eardrums. 'I've got to see you. You've got to let me. Anytime. Tell me anytime you're free.'

'Well, you're certainly in your bossyboots today, but, I don't know, I don't know baby.' — Again a pause — 'Where are you? Can you talk?'

The secretary, advancing down the corridor, had spotted the intruder in her office. Pattie snatched the phone off the desk and huddled over it in the corner. 'Yes. Fine. Talk.'

'Its not a good idea, little bird. You don't know any lesbians except me. You ought to meet some nice women, young women who read books, your kind of people. Go down to the club again — take that beetle-browed girlfriend of yours if you like, but not the curb-crawling voyeur creep — and get to know people.

You're a dear thing and quite smart. People will take you to their hearts. You'll find a real world there.'

Pattie nodded briefly to the secretary who was easing herself into her typing chair with a sigh, and bent down again over the phone. 'There's only one world that's real; that's what I want to see you about.'

'Come on now! Use your pumpkin head.'

'I love you.'

'Yes-yes-yes. Love me: hate my fucking; scares you rigid. How's that for a formula for mental health?'

'Could I come over and talk about it?'

'We're talking now. I can't do it any other way, baby; it's what I've had since I was five years old, my daddy's personal gift. If you weren't so damn bossy, I wouldn't have to say all this, but, well. Look chicken: you couldn't conceive of the bloody mess my life is. Can you even imagine the people I mix with? Think you could bring your girlfriend round to tea with me? She'd turn against you, you know; she'd be jealous and hurt and ashamed. Maybe she'd understand if you got to be a nice lesbian; but with me? She'd wash herself clean of you. She'd broadcast technicolour stories all over the school.'

Eugenie, who had been so good to her, would now be waiting, refining the list for a picnic that would never take place. Because Pattie was going to abandon her and take the heart out of her world. Pattie would not deny her some just revenge.

'And you know — you're still there? — what that leads to? The most disgusting men will be turned on by it and persecute you with slavering. School — you'd have to write off school. And do you think I'd be nice to you while you were going through all this? Think I'd help you? Five minutes of it would bore me stiff.'

'It would?' There was the beginnings of something like triumph in the furious beat of Pattie's heart.

'And me; have you thought of me? What happens to me when you get bored with the ordinary middle-aged woman you'll try to turn me into? What then, little bird?'

The bell rang. 'We'll take it one day at a time,' Pattie yelled over the din. 'And I'm coming over now. I'll go sick for this afternoon.'

'Oh God, I'm not even awake yet. I'd give my tits for a cup of camomile tea. I'll pick you up after school. But no promises you understand. Where do you live—and what's your name again?'

Head high, Pattie marched towards the science hut. 'I'm Patricia Monica Symons,' she said out loud, 'and I'm going to fight and I hope one day to win.'

In the scale of the vaulted corridor, she seemed a very small figure.

Mondi

In the middle of nowhere, the school bus screeched to a halt. A rather scruffy, mouse-haired girl tumbled out. She shook herself straight, shuffling in boots that seemed to be made of lead.

'Satchel!' she shouted.

An arm reached out through the window and tossed a hide bag with a big iron buckle.

'*Dankie.*' She hauled the bag onto her shoulder and lifted a khaki beret.

'Make speed Hennie', somebody yelled from the bus in his rumbling Afrikaans language. 'There's gonna be a *donder-'n-blitzen* of a storm.'

That was no lie. Hennie lifted her head and smelt the thick wetness of the wind. The gold had gone out in her father's maizefields and the sky was shutting down against the mountains. Soon lightning would crack itself against the peaks and then a wave of wind and hail and water would wash out the world. 'Ja, Ja,' she called back gaily, and waved until the bus lurched off.

She walked, not, as one would expect, up the track to the van Rensberg farm, but across the veld to a clump of thorn trees. The storm would break in at best half an hour, but Hennie was not afraid.

Mondi and the pony would be waiting for her beneath the trees. Mondi had no fear of storms. Nor, when she was with Mondi, had the pony — called Intusi because her forehead blaze was white as milk. Maybe they would race to beat the storm; maybe they would huddle it out; maybe they would just charge through it. Mondi would know which. Though not afraid, Hennie was a little excited, partly by the sudden cooling and the wind running waves through the grass, but mainly because the best moment of all the day was coming soon. She would pull off her boot and caliper and Mondi would help her onto Intusi's bare back. Then her poor, soft, unmade foot would curl back into its mouse-shape and be comfortable; then, doubled up with Mondi on Intusi, she could outrun any girl anywhere.

Hennie was the only child of Martinus van Rensberg, whose family had farmed here in Natal, in the stony foothills of the Drakensberg Mountains, for more than a hundred years. They, the van Rensbergs — shoulder to shoulder with the giants — the Pretoriuses, the Retiefs, the Maritzes — had fulfilled the Bible's prophecy and taken this land from the Zulus by force of arms. Their triumph, though, was short, for the Queen of England had sent regiments of redcoats and traitorous African clans against them and they, like the Zulus, were defeated. But not totally and not for ever: they had kept their language, religion and, what really mattered, the land. And now, in the 1950s, they were running the government. The Bible had not been wrong. But, typical of this false world, they had no money; the rednecks in their posh cities kept that for themselves.

Hennie's father, in his rare light moments, liked to stand on the stoep, legs splayed, with his pipe and his brandy, chatting to the oldest of his farmhands about these things. They, leaning on their knobkerries in the yard, and smoking pipes of even stronger tobacco, remembered their own stories of the Boers pouring down the mountains with their covered wagons and herds of skinny cattle. Those herds had been much improved when the Zulu cattle was added to them.

'You see *Bomadala*,' Hennie's father would say, 'we brought you law and civilization. We stopped you killing each other. Now you can all have thirty cows and buy yourselves nice fat wives, heh!'

And the old men would chuckle and wait until the baas had had enough brandy to be in the mood to bring out a jug of the fiery stuff for them to pass round. They always changed the subject if he started talking about the future, because then his jovial mood — and with it the promise of brandy — would vanish.

The baas had a big strong wife who could make wonderful mealiebread and vetkoek; but she, who should have borne seven sons, had given him only this one half-child, a girl who would not grow straight enough to get herself a man who had served in the army and could run the farm. They knew that the baas tried hard not to notice that she was only a girl. Perhaps, even, because she was not a proper girl, he could pretend she was a boy and would be able to do man's work, run the farm: she, who would never wield a sjambok, whom nobody would bother to obey, who could not even do women's work like hoeing and weeding; a soft girl who took no pleasure in hunting even though she could ride a horse pretty well. They thought of their own sons and grandsons powerful as mules and working in the gold mines, and they pitied the baas with all their hearts.

Martinus van Rensberg never spoke to the old men about his family. He spoke about the government's promise to give more help to farmers. He spoke about the new education system which would close down the poverty-stricken mission schools and give the *Bomadala*'s grandchildren teaching in useful things like cattle dipping and bantu crafts. He spoke about the black men in Pietermaritzburg who wore spats and waistcoats and pretended to read newspapers, and the old men agreed that this was shocking.

None the less, they knew all about the troubles of the van Rensburg family. They knew that the missis was waiting for her maiden auntie to die to get a hundred pounds for an operation on Hennie's club foot. They knew that the baas owed the government more money than his farm was worth. They knew that the brandy they would be drinking was cheap rough stuff, a white man's drink, but only just.

Mondi, as usual, was sitting under the tree writing in the dust with her long fingers. The pony, untethered, was munching grass a few feet away. Hennie looked at Mondi's thin black shoulders, hunched over the work, her legs, stretched out before her, ending in two perfectly-made dust-stained feet. She went up close; she read the English words:

'I go. I went. I will go. I have gone. I had gone. I was going. I will have gone.'

'When do you say "I gone" Hennitjie?' said Mondi without looking up.

'When you've finished going, I guess', said Hennie uncertainly. 'I dunno. I hate English. It's a stupid language. I dunno why they have to make up such complicated ways of saying things instead of saying them straight.'

As if in agreement, a long, low growl of thunder rolled down from the mountains. Before the pony had even lifted its head to whinny, Mondi was on her feet and, catching the dangling reins, had led it in under the bushes.

'Shush-shu-shu,' she told Intusi, 'the lightning's still miles away.'

Hennie watched with pleasure, knowing that soon she would be on the pony's back, clinging to her mane, Mondi's powerful knees holding them firm against the rocking canter, the rush of wind, the rain thowing itself at them. But first there was an important ritual. She tossed the satchel to Mondi. 'Have a look.'

Mondi undid the big iron buckle with care and drew out two, three dog-eared books. Her brows, almost always serious, were furrowed. '*A Christmas Carol* by Charles Dickens': she pronounced the words carefully. After wiping her hands a second time on her vest, she opened the pages and stared at the small, dense print. 'Man, this is real English, hey Hennitjie,' she said.

'Ja man. We started it this week. It's hellava hard. It's called a novel.'

'Its got two names?'

'No man, a novel means a story, a long one that's really hard. D'ya wanna try it? That, there at the bottom, that's a dictionary, a proper one.'

Mondi shook her head. 'If it's hard for you, it's no good for me. I'll stick with your geography book, and your biology — that's the best one. I've been trying to remember since yesterday which one of a snake's lungs is the big one. Can I look?'

Hennie nodded tersely. She sat down to wait while Mondi

peered at the pages, and began to unbuckle her boots.

Hennie was nearly thirteen, two or perhaps three years Mondi's junior, and any stupid could see that she was beginning to outstrip Mondi in learning. The shame of this was that to Mondi learning mattered so much. It was one of those dumb things because Mondi couldn't do anything with learning even if she got it. She would never get a pass* to look for a reading-and-writing job in town; she was too useful on the farm where she belonged. And the new government had promised to do much more to help farmers keep their good labour. Mondi knew all that; there was no point in telling her. And what was dumber than dumb was that learning didn't matter to anybody else, certainly not to Hennie's father who seemed almost ashamed that Hennie did fairly well at school — it reminded him that she was a girl. In Mondi's studies Meneer van Rensberg took a slight interest, once giving Mondi a tickey** when she moved up a grade.

Mondi had started working for the van Rensburgs when she was about seven. Because she was lanky and tended to drop things, she was used out in the kitchen garden and didn't ordinarily come to the house. It was chance that brought the girls together. Hennie's mother had seen Mondi among the cabbages, making little clay cattle that seemed almost alive. So she had brought her into the yard to amuse her whimpering child, and she rewarded her services with a *koeksister* every Saturday. Hennie whined much less after that and even seemed to grow a little. Mondi too had gained — and more than cookies — for, at about age nine she was taken on to help clean the stables. And there she showed such a knack with horses that she was allowed time off on Mondays and Thursdays to attend the afternoon shifts at the mission school a few miles away. She was allowed to ride the pony to school in exchange for collecting Hennie from the school bus afterwards. Mondi, Meneer van Rensberg said,

---

* *Pass: a document black people over age sixteen had to acquire to be allowed to live and work outside the area to which the state had assigned them.*
** *Three pence*

sometimes a little resentfully, was the most privileged girl on the farm. Then Mondi, who had been stony-faced even as a little child, put on the deep frown which turned her old well beyond her years, but said nothing in reply.

Mondi, Hennie and Intusi often roamed on the way home. Hennie, wanting the rides to go on forever, delayed the end by any means possible. They had ridden through many summer storms before. They had been all over the farm and beyond — down to the river, up to the waterfall at the foot of the mountains, and to Mondi's home, a little cluster of round mud huts, thatched, and painted with lime and red clay slip. There they had watched Mondi's little brothers and sisters making clay figures (not cattle, but guns and tanks). Mondi's mother worked till late and had no money for a kerosene lamp, so sometimes on the dark winter evenings the two girls had seized their chance and drunk the sour kaffir beer until they were awash with giggles and Intusi had to find the way back to the farmhouse.

But they had never been to the mission together. Hennie was frightened of nuns, these foreign white women who moved about like boats in their funny clothes, and ate Jesus, and lived with blacks, and caused trouble on the farms. She knew that Mondi thought the world of them, so she kept this to herself. But she also knew that the mission school had hardly any exercise books or pencils, so she shared hers with Mondi — as far as she could without being caught.

Mondi looked up from the book. 'Frogs and snakes grow lungs; that's easy, but English really is hard, isn't it Hennitjie,' she said.

'Ja. And English people, you know, they talk ever so fast and clippy, like birds, like they were chewing tobacco really fast. I've seen them, you know, the doctors at the hospital in Pietermaritzburg talking about my foot. Hellava stupid hey.'

'Really, man?' Mondi had never been to Underberg, let alone Pietermaritzburg, but she had heard the nuns speaking French among themselves — sweet pure voices rising and twining like birdsong — and now that she had entered the third grade,

English classes had begun. These were solemn tones, full of power: 'I go; I will go; I went', and, her mouth watering with the tension of separating out the breathy sounds, the magnificent 'I will have gone'. Mondi could speak and write Zulu, Xhosa and Afrikaans and sing (without understanding a word) the whole of the Latin Mass. To her there was nothing especially strange about people talking like birds chewing tobacco; the Tower of Babel was completely natural — cows talked a different language from goats — the world was not made to fit just her head. 'Hellava hard, Hennitjie.'

'Anyway,' she added — carefully testing the strength of the much-repaired spine of the biology book and then tucking it back into the satchel — 'I guess we'd better get moving or the books'll get wet.'

She laced Hennie's boots to the satchel, slung it over her shoulder, lifted Hennie onto the pony's back and, with a loud 'Chip-chip', vaulted up herself and they were away. Waves of wind rattled through the maize, bent the long grass double and roared in Hennie's ears. Intusi's hard hooves thumped, her powerful shoulders and lungs working like a great engine. Hennie grasped the mane and turned the pony firmly towards the mountains, towards the storm: 'Make speed, Intusi, fly,' she yelled, and yelled again as the pony responded and Mondi's arms tightened against the change of pace. The thunder, like the long low growling of a wild animal, was becoming more frequent.

But after too few minutes, Mondi was reaching round her, gentling the pony and directing them back towards the rutted track to the farmhouse. As they slowed, Hennie felt a few great wet drops against her face.

The storm broke as they reached the yard. Sheets of water whooshed over them, and they were soaked in a second. Mondi leapt off the pony to drop the satchel, boots dangling, in the shelter of the stoep. Then she carried Hennie across, ran Intusi to the stable and sprinted back. They had to rush to put back Hennie's boot and caliper; Hennie hated her father to see her without her boots on. So far, nobody had noticed their arrival.

Then came the hail, making the crash of a thousand drums on the tin roof. Hailstones ricocheting in the yard spattered them as they struggled with the boot. The gushing rain, mist closing in and steam rising from the warm earth walled off the outside world. Mondi's shiny black hair was full of hailstones, like a cherry tree in blossom. Pebbles of ice and great drops of water fell into Hennie's lap as Mondi leant over her, wiping the water off her foot, cold and curled up like a sleeping mouse, pressing the foot back into its iron and leather prison. She paid no attention when Hennie winced, but firmly buckled the caliper over the khaki sock and fastened the laces.

Then she stood back, water streaming down her body and over her beautiful feet, and waited while Hennie struggled out of the chair and began to limp up and down — the first steps were always hurt a bit more.

'I reckon Pa's home, man,' Hennie said, putting off the moment of opening the door. She pictured her father standing at the window, arms folded tight across his rifle, peering into the mist in case cattle thieves should try to use the storm for cover.

'Reckon so,' replied Mondi, 'with all this rain.' Unsmiling as ever, she picked up the satchel and held it out for Hennie.

Hennie took a deep breath. She could feel her blood pounding in time with the hail. She looked at Mondi and saw her as other people did — a scrawny black girl with no shoes wearing a soaking-wet ragged vest and skirt made out of mealbags. Water was dripping off her chin, nose and ears and she made no attempt to wipe it away. Hennie was suddenly enraged at the stupidness of it all.

'*Ag*, that useless thing', she said, lungeing at the satchel and striking it with her fist, 'I don't want that stupid thing. You take it away.'

'What? This?' Mondi gave a brief joyless laugh. 'Are you going mad or something?'

'Ja, keep it — *A Christmas Carol* and the English dictionary and the biology and the maths set; keep the damn lot.'

Now Mondi was shocked. She stepped back, and Hennie felt herself swamped with a terrible need to cry. She stood hard on her bad foot, bringing on the sharp and familiar pain that always brought her to her senses. Her tone changed. 'Yes, please keep it Mondi,' she said. 'Go on. It's what I want. I'll tell them I lost it in the storm. But keep it at the mission or they'll say you stole it.'

'*Ag*, no man. You know you can't. It doesn't belong to you; it belongs to the baas. I know there isn't any money to buy another one. You can't do such a thing. It'd be a sin.'

'What do I need it for?' cried Hennie. 'I'm going to be a bankrupt farmer, like my Pa. He can't speak English. He can't read novels. What use is it for me to be different? Hey?' And, after a pause, 'Go on Mondi, I want you to take it.'

'*Ag*, no man,' repeated Mondi. 'You don't have to try to be a farmer. You could maybe even be a schoolteacher one day. *Ag* hell no, no, never.' But Mondi's voice suddenly broke, giving away her excitement. Recognizing the signal, they burst into a laugh at the same moment.

It was done.

Hennie nodded brusquely and went into the house.

'Hennitjie, is it you?' Her mother's voice from the kitchen rose above the sound of the hail, thinning now. 'Come here and dry out by the stove. You'll get a terrible cold. They should've kept you at school.'

'What d'ya mean Ma?' boomed her father's voice, 'They don't keep other children at school when there's a few drops of rain. The girl won't melt; you're turning her into a damn sissy.'

Hennie's left shoulder felt oddly light, as if, satchel-less, it was lifting up into the air. 'Coming Ma,' she said.

But she didn't go directly. She peered through the mosquito netting, to see Mondi take off her tattered vest, wrap the satchel against the rain as if it was a living baby, and let herself out into the mist.

Mondi is a Xhosa name (also used by Zulus in southern Natal), which means 'patience' and 'fortitude'. In many African literatures, the quality of patience is associated with powerful hunting animals which must wait quietly, even when they are very hungry, for the right moment to attack. 'With patience and endurance, the falcon gets its prey' — Twi proverb from Ghana.

After the Party

Charlene looked up from the pool of red wine, slanting of its own accord in the glass, at a night where, beyond the dishevelled curtains, soft white flakes were tilting into other glass.

'...Best new party idea since they invented twelfth night, isn't it, Charlie?'

The waves of Deirdre's voice swirled up to her and struck, as at a sea wall. My lover's big red mouth, Charlene thought, will go on churning all night.

'...And then, my little Sir Charles, in February we'll throw another party to celebrate the start of the salmon season.'

Deirdre was sprawled on the settee, the heels of her boots anchored into its soft blue fabric. As she planned the next parties, her little Siamese cat scuttled, crablike, among the debris of the one which had just ended. He scratched through rugs for anchovies and olives, picked at plates strewn over the guitar, slithered over the records on the floor. All this, Charlene thought, will go on churning all night.

'...Our friends adore my salmon poached in a little vermouth,' Deirdre continued, 'old greedy guts Octavius — did you notice last time I did it, he had three helpings?' Deirdre's arms, high above her head, sketched mountainous plates of salmon in the air. Charlene watched the moving hands, recalling Deirdre's disappointment when Octavius resisted her entreaties to a fourth helping. 'I'll get a big one' — her arms opened wider to measure a salmon the size of a barracuda; 'I'll invite ten seamen's appetites, make it a salmon festival; I'll put that gorgeous new oven you bought me under full steam.'

Charlene tilted the red pool the other way. 'We're on an overdraft,' she said dully.

'Oh Charlie, be bold: there is a tide in the affairs of men, remember, which, taken at the full, leads on to — '

As the familiar waves of panic rose in her chest, Charlene lunged at the space above her in a desperate effort to haul her body off the floor; she achieved a half-sitting position. ' — On to bankruptcy', she spat. 'We're drowning in — Oh shit!' Charlene stared at a red puddle down between her knees, oozing across the white carpet. 'You made me spill my bloody wine,' she muttered.

Deirdre, who had thrown tonight's party largely to celebrate the new carpet, contemplated with tranquility the spreading stain. 'Heap a pack of salt on it,' she said. 'That's best for red wine. And I won't have you swearing, Carlus, makes you sound common.'

Salt. Common. Not the point. 'You didn't even wait till we'd paid for that carpet before getting it ruined,' Charlene wailed, looking up into a face plump and serene as a Buddha. She wrenched her glance free; it fell first on the rumpled rugs, softly rising and falling, then on a lampshade glistening like a bobbing buoy, then on snowflakes hurling themselves to suicide against the window; her eyes trawled the room for something, some order, to cling to. A deep breath, deep as you could breathe of air toasted biscuit-dry by the boiler raging in the kitchen.

She was bursting: 'I'm not Charles This or Sir Carlus That, I'm Charlene.'

No. Missed. That wasn't what she was going to say. She hated the very sound of that soft, drippy, ridiculous name, bolted onto her like a drag-queen's padded bra. That was one of the things you only said to get yourself in a rage with the whole bloody world, start a row with the mouth on the settee. She didn't want to start what could only end with her tough self in snivels; she wanted to throw things, to throw out into the snow the echoes of those eight guzzling, boozing, bawling voices that had flooded her home for six hours. She wanted to dry up her lover's mouth, sew up her pockets. 'I'm Charlene and proud.' She stared fiercely at the plates of her feet (focusing hard to reduce their number from four to two) — her very own big, flat, common, salty feet that knew how to kick. 'And I'm too proud to be flash with money I haven't got.'

She was being stupid. Deirdre didn't spill the wine. Deirdre hadn't made her stretch her Visacard to its limit to buy the cooker, forced the business to bear the cost of the white carpet. She'd agreed with Deirdre that that ghastly name was best buried. The enemy was closer to home, swirling inside her own thick head. To find, somewhere, some order. She turned and hissed at the cat to get his claws out of her Tracy Chapman records.

It was almost exactly two years now since that fateful night, that night that came out of nothing, out of the fog. Charlene had pulled up on the M25 (between the festoons of roadworks) when she saw two women flapping about over a steaming radiator. Only a cretin could get into that kind of trouble in the depths of winter. It had taken Charlene five minutes by torchlight and a pair of tights whipped off one of the women's bottoms to get the car going again. Then, at a tedious 40 miles an hour, she had convoyed them safely home to Kentish Town. Afterwards, perhaps just to entertain herself by wiping the gush off their faces and putting in its place a touch of anxiety, a touch of greed, she had driven off in their much-abused car, laughing to herself at two nobs who couldn't resist a free service but would now be wondering if they'd ever see their car again. She'd taken it back to Ilford, where she sorted out the fan, tidied up a few bits and pieces (like the muckiest spark plugs you ever saw) and returned it, as appointed, Tuesday at dawn.

That was when she noticed that the dishier of these two women was giving her the eye.

Now this was something you didn't refuse, the signal every motor mechanic waited for. Especially when the dishy one sent the other packing off to work. Too bad about the filling station, where Billie would be waiting for her to open the service bay. Charlene wiped her oily hands on a towel while her mouth watered for somewhere warmer and wetter to put them.

'Coffee?'
'Ta.'

Deirdre had made coffee quite unlike any coffee Charlene had known before, such a rush of hot steam, such a richness of big, juicy, freshly-roasted beans, such silky cream curling round in the cup. Charlene, seated by Deirdre in the big upholstered chair, spread legs encased in greasy overalls, making herself at ease.

She had done well that morning, she told Billie when she reached the station two hours late. The imprint of her thumb she had left, in black grease, on Deirdre's chin.

'You're not listening, my little Carlus.' Charlene jerked herself back to the room. 'Of course you're proud. And I loathe money too — filthy, vulgar stuff — don't want to have anything to do with it. And I'm proud of you, so proud. Every time I show you off to our friends, I think: could any of them have risen from grease monkey to garage manager in two years? And done it all by themselves?'

By themselves? It was Deirdre who had booked her into night school to learn accounts; Deirdre who had raked the BP garage inventory for a station unattractive enough to be available to a woman; Deirdre who had chosen the run-down place at Catford. And, during that terrifying setting-up period, Deirdre's imagination had blossomed with brilliant business ideas. She had got the local wino, for a few bob, to clear the broken glass and rubble off the edges of the forecourt. She had figured that if you accepted every credit card in the book, you'd lighten the load of cash in the till. And that if you banked the takings every two hours you could risk refusing protection offers from the Catford Tigers, the police, the local security firms.

Charlene didn't want all this swimming in her head. After all, it was also Deirdre who had given up her job the better to be able to help with Charlene's, and who would now view with complacency the lengthening columns of Charlene's debts, the swelling mountains of their possessions. 'It's coming along fine.' Deirdre would say, 'Now just increase turnover by 20 per cent a year for five years and we'll be laughing.' (Apart from that, Deirdre no longer took any interest in the business.)

'All by myself,' Charlene lied.

'All by your tough butch beautiful little self.'

As this compliancy — composed how much of mockery? — trickled into her consciousness, Charlene lifted her eyes to a mouth breaking now into a big, slow, enveloping smile. Not good enough. She wasn't going to be mollified until she'd done it all by herself, made Deirdre say it out loud: 'Charlene.' (And, if she could just get her thoughts and her limbs together, there were other problems — she should rescue the guitar, replace the broken manhole cover on the forecourt; there was something urgent to do with salt.) Taking a deep breath, she yelled again at the cat.

'We'll always be proud, Charlie my babe,' Deirdre's smile softened as the little cat, tail folded close under his stomach, slunk to safety under the arch of her legs. 'And when we're old, just you and me, we'll cling valiantly together and sing — ' Deirdre's mouth rounded as she shaped it for song — '"We had fun, while it lasted, We had fun".'

Deirdre had a remarkable singing voice, big and gutsy, slightly cracked from hitting hard against the walls of the world. She could sing like a soldier on the march, like Ethel Merman in *Gypsy*, like a lady in furs hollering hymns from the deck of the Titanic. 'We had fun.'

This was the song Deirdre had sung at so many parties at that Kentish Town flat crammed with creaky antiques, in the small hours, when the couples and the careerwomen had gone home, and of those left only Deirdre was still on her feet. Then she had filled her great lungs and boomed out, accompanied by the electronic whine of a milkfloat in the street.

The first party was only a few days after Charlene returned the car. Charlene, inside a clean houndstooth check suit and throttled by a bow-tie, with her neck still red from the barber's razor, had arrived nervous. But she knew she was all right as soon as Deirdre opened the door: inked on her chin in black eyeliner was a big beauty spot, exactly where Charlene's thumb-print had been.

Deirdre, arms wide, had ushered in 'the young chevalier who galloped in on a white charger to rescue us stranded on the motorway.' And the women there, leaning on the mantelpiece and downing astonishing quantities of whisky as they talked soberly about their cats, their illnesses, their ex-lovers and their therapists, had paused and smiled — approval, perhaps, of Deirdre's chevalier. Charlene had her place.

And she had enjoyed it. Among those tired worldweighted lives, only she had the freedom to be coarse, be camp, be young, be cheap; be the one bright point of flame in a dying grate. There Charlene discovered the small difference between these smart women and a motor mechanic who tussled with her mates at clubs and her birds in the back seat of her car: Deirdre's cronies acted as if all of life could be charged to the company account. And she soon found that they were just as hungry and wanting as real people, and that she had something they were hungry for. It seemed to her that any of those women would have fixed her up for a night at the Savoy, if she'd given the nod. And it was clear to her that Deirdre thought this too and was flattered by it.

Charlene, by then wearing casuals from Austin Reed chosen for her by Deirdre, felt herself swell with pride at her lover's pride in her new possession. Gallantly, she flirted with Deirdre's middle-aged friends and laughed with them when they laughed at the order in which she laid out the knives and forks. And she thought of that delicious later, when they would have gone and Deirdre's other woman passed out, leaving two souls to roll free on a hearthrug still pitted from expensive boots. Charlene had no complaints about this affair. Nor, it would seem, had Deirdre, who would drive to the station just about every day, the car loaded with gifts, for Charlene to cram another half-gallon of petrol into the tank.

But Deirdre had become restless. She wanted more. She spoke about her loneliness and her wasted life. She froze out the old chums who called Charlene 'Lennie'. She took to dropping in at Ilford, even making laughable attempts to charm Charlene's landlady. With her other woman — who was, after all, not always smashed out of her brains — Deirdre took crazy risks of disclosure. She took Charlene off for a weekend at Bognor where she talked of eloping to Seychelles. Then she began to talk about marriage, plan a future. 'You're keen, you're tough, my little shark, you have so much potential; you can make you and me a wonderful new world.' Charlene the motor mechanic had watched uneasily her metamorphosis into Charles the knight in shining armour.

But then, one evening in a restaurant — when the waiter had (with no signal from Deirdre) poured the tasting wine into Charlene's glass — Charlene had looked boldly at this big expensive woman who looked at her with soft eyes and she thought: 'Yes, I can do it. Now I have Deirdre, I can do anything I want.' And so she had gone to night school, and bid for and got BP's worst filling station; she had paid for Deirdre in advance. That was, she sometimes thought, the only bill she had met in full.

As Deirdre sang, Charlene looked at her round, moist lips, at the sinews straining in her throat, at the breasts lifting with each breath. She remembered, how, the first time she had watched Deirdre sing, she had been pained by the marks, outlined on Deirdre's silk dress, of the brassiére cutting into flesh. She had stared at her across a room weighted with ageing women, longing to loosen the armour and free those heavy breasts to fall against her face. Now Charlene knew what she'd been getting in such a fuss about. 'Let's forget all this mess,' she said. 'Let's go to bed.'

To bed, where bills could become so much lavatory paper on a spike, where two bodies, a cat and a duvet comprised the world. Yes, to bed, where Deirdre let all her wildness be rolled up by Charlene into one great ball, charging deeper and deeper into space, where Charlene would strain, frantic to break into that wonderful strong body, till Deirdre's breath came harder and faster and then broke in loud, long wails, Charlene's little cries mixing with them as they waned.

'Oh please! Now.' Charlene was up on her feet, dragging at the inert mass of her lover's body. Then, again, but crossly, 'Oh, come on: now!'

Deirdre didn't budge. 'Course I want you madly, you little

piece of rough,' she said, 'but come lie quiet in my arms for a moment; I'm a bit half seas over.'

As Deirdre's bare white arms opened wide, and her legs shifted slightly to nudge the little cat into a more protected position, Charlene registered a putdown. And somewhere in that, a double meaning. She got it: Deirdre, on whom the only effect of wine seemed to be to make her, if possible, even sexier, was gently reminding Charlene of the several times Charlene had rushed her to bed after a party and zonked out in the middle of the first kiss. The wave of anger which had broken into desire fell back into the beginnings of a new anger. Charlene carefully sidestepped this feeling; she could be devious too. She ignored the outstretched arms and, folding her own, looked down at her lover, pinned there on the couch. 'I fancy you when you're pissed.' Then she watched as the real meaning of that hit the spot.

'Yes, Charlie my darling. These days you only fancy me when I'm pissed.'

Shit. Why was she doing this? Of course she was fed up with endless boring parties; she was worried sick about money. But there was nothing wrong between her and Deirdre. Or was there? When last had she, sober, desired Deirdre, beautiful, womanly, vulnerable Deirdre?

'Come on. Say,' said Deirdre softly. Truth time; the hour before dawn. Your Deirdre's a big girl. Just say it.'

The snow, slushier now, was still flopping against the window. Charlene thought very carefully, then said: 'I like you — ' she paused. Last chance to pull back. No, with a flutter of expectation, she realized that something was coming which had waited a long time to be born. Something had changed between them perhaps a year ago, yet they had both gone on pretending that she, Charlene, was no more than Deirdre's little protege, led by the hand through the world. She would not pull back. As power surged through her, she let it out slowly: ' — I like you when I hurt you.'

Deirdre laughed. 'Oh, Sir Charles, then you must like me a lot of the time.'

Charlene's slow glance took in a face which had fallen into the contours of middle age. 'Must I? Oh God, I'm sorry.'

'Sorry? It's what you meant. It's all right. I know it anyway.' A tender smile spread over Deirdre's face. 'I know you're going off me. Soon, maybe quite soon — maybe tomorrow, or the next day — there'll be somebody else, somebody young, dainty, pretty. She'll be mad about you. You'll drive her wild with your lovemaking, you know little Carlus, because I taught you so well.' She paused. 'We'll have a few dramas, you and me. But not many. You won't be terribly interested in quarrelling. You'll just want out. That's the way you'll leave me. But it's all right, little Prince Charles. We'll have had fun.'

'No, hang on —' Standing straighter, Charlene struggled for clarity. What was this thing that was happening? She wanted to fuck, not fight. She loved Deirdre. Deirdre was beautiful. Deirdre had given her a new life. 'You mustn't manage me like you do, like a child,' she said. 'I don't want to play that game any more. When I give you pain, I'm on top; I unseat you; I can see you're not made of marble. It's the only time.'

'O Charlie, you don't know your own strength.'

'I'm beginning to know. And I want use it to start again. I don't want you to choose my shirts, hold dozens of stupid dinner parties. That's not what I want.'

'I only do it for you.' said Deirdre slowly. 'Perhaps it's all I have to give.'

Charlene was remorseless. She didn't know where it came from, but there was something she had to get straight. 'It's not what I want. I'm not a paper doll of the Prince of Wales. Can't you see? I'm not some kind of bin you shovel salmon into. I'm Charlene — Charlene who wants to screw with you. Now.'

Deirdre sat up. 'But you love salmon. The first time I did it for you — at Kentish Town, remember — you were over the moon; you'd never tasted it before, except out of a tin. God, you were funny that night, in your awful clothes that smelled of the launderette. Oh Charlie, you were the sweetest thing, the dearest, chirpiest, ballsiest little shrimp.' Deirdre's eyes were moist with feeling. 'We'll have one more glass of this lovely rioja. We'll have fun, something to remember when it's all over. Pour for us both, baby Carlus, and come drink it lying in my arms.'

After the Party

Charlene's struggles to aim the wine into the gyrating loop of space in the middle of the glasses as quickly as possible so that she could dive into her lover's body and settle the whole thing right there on the couch, did not take up the whole of her mind. In its eddies it scoffed at its mean little centre; its fear of living, laughing, loving to the full like Deirdre could show her how. If only Deirdre, who had taught her so much, could teach her how to be good to Deirdre.

'I so love this moment, Charlie' — Deirdre's fingers ran over the cropped surface of Charlene's hair as Charlene reached under the shirt to fight with bra-fastenings trapped deep beneath a heavy back — 'When I have my own dear love in my arms; when I see total trust in the big blue eyes of my little cat; when I've had a gorgeous evening and sent eight troubled people home contented and full of good food; when I'm in my own precious home that my Carlus built, which all our friends love to visit because every room radiates warmth and love. This is what life is for.'

Charlene, fumbling now to drag her lover's trousers down to the knees, noted the imperfectly drawn curtains and, in real satisfaction, decided to let the world go hang. Hardly able to wait for the tingle of Deirdre's fingers teasing the nerves running down her back, she yanked off her shirt, and, bare-chested, threw a stare at the sleety window: let anyone who dared make mock of her and her beautiful lover. Let anyone who dared say that they would soon, perhaps quite soon, be splitting up.

Deirdre was still romantic. 'I love our home madly, Charlie, just as it is,' she said dreamily, 'but I'd so adore a dining room.' The tiny pearl buttons on Deirdre's shirt were causing problems. 'Bellamy Antiques has the most gorgeous Victorian set,' Deirdre said, watching Charlene's fumbling fingers. 'Eight chairs, one a carver just made for you, and beautiful french polishing on the table. I can just see the salmon laid out on it. All our friends will love it.'

'I'll send Billie round with the truck to pick it up in the morning.' Charlene's voice rose, muffled, from a mouth pressed into her lover's throat. 'Help me loosen this button.'

Overnighting at De Aar

Mrs Raikes leaned her back against the car, stretching long arms over the dusty curve of its roof. 'I do love this Highveld wind,' she said. 'So inorganic.'

Obedient to her wishes, a little squall sprang up, charging, a ball of fluffy red dust, over the veld, through the buds of the cosmos flowers fringing the road, up to the thorn tree and the shiny black Bentley parked, at a crazy angle, underneath. It nudged the tongues of her shoes, played with the hem of her tweed skirt, then tugged at her heavy iron-grey hair.

'So different, Lilian my dear, from the winds of Europe, which smell of decay.'

Lilian Naidoo, crouched over a little paraffin stove under the tree, shielded its flame. 'Don't these winds,' she said, 'smell of those two Special Branch men just around the corner, peeing in the culvert?'

Mrs Raikes sniffed. 'Well, we are roughly downwind of them. But, no. Africa's Gods are not sentimental. They give the prey no favour over the hunter. Just crack your lips, break your back, blind you with the glare. Simple. Clean.' She stretched again. 'Fetch me a cigarette, dear girl, from the glove compartment. This is a continent without emotion. Every quivering duiker accepts that; it's fools like you and me who bleat about intercession.'

While Lilian's fingers felt about the dark space for the lighter she knew so well as a cool metal smoothness fondled in another pair of hands, broad hands with square-cut fingernails, surprisingly clean for the hands of a white person, Mrs Raikes called out again: 'Would it be wicked to suggest just the smallest nip from the hip flask in there?' Lilian's fingers found the flask. 'Would that be regarded as undermining your sensible suggestion of a stop for tea to refresh two women of experience staring at a thousand miles of road?'

'A thousand miles with them in the rear-view mirror? Yes, you could call it sabotage — but a wonderful idea.'

Lilian let the door click gently to and went round to the other side. Mrs Raikes, still leaning against the car body, was easing her back with little movements of the shoulders: so deliberate a statement of relaxedness must surely be aimed at the two men behind. Was Mrs Raikes actually enjoying this chase? With a spurt of alarm, Lilian saw on her companion's face that cool temerity of Europeans, people too accustomed to mastery to take wholly seriously the holster bulging on the hip.

'I think you despise them,' she said, 'too much to fear them.'

'They bore me.' Mrs Raikes sniffed again. 'And I think you were right; they have fouled the wind.'

Lilian returned her companion's wry smile. Mrs Raikes looked a little tired. The dust had dried the sweat off her face, deepening the fine cracks in her lips, leaving dampness only where grey curls still stuck to her forehead and a delicate curve of cheekbone just in front of her ear.

'Perhaps,' Lilian offered gamely, 'a continent gives its emotion only to the people who belong to it, the people who make a language with a dozen words for the different rednesses of its earth.'

'Your mental energy amazes me, dear girl. For myself I doubt if I have the strength even to reach for that cigarette.'

At a safe distance of some three paces, Lilian picked one out of the pack and, rather awkwardly, tested the lighter. Mrs Raikes watched, her fingers tapping against shiny black paint. Quickly and seriously, Lilian judged the distance, crossed the gap, put the cigarette between the other woman's lips, and fired the lighter. Then she stepped back, almost flinching from the sting of a need to look into her face.

'Ah,' she heard Mrs Raikes say with satisfaction, 'what pleasure could be greater than this?'

The two women of experience did indeed face a formidable stretch of road. Trailed from the start by the grey Toyota of the security police, they had left Johannesburg in the morning, planning to drive hard and fast, to overnight at De Aar, and reach Cape Town before the next evening, when Mrs Raikes would need to be fresh enough to speak to a roomful of women students about the Black Sash.

Her job would not be as easy one. The women's organization she represented, founded in the fifties to mourn the 'death of the constitution' when people of mixed race were disenfranchised, was now burdened with a tired, middle-aged, middle-class image. Patiently, it picked up the casualties of a long smouldering war, feeding destitute people banished to the desert for their work in trade unions, supporting the families of political prisoners, demonstrating with perfect manners against each new law, insisting always on the power of a partnership of women to confront violence with nothing more potent than disapproval.

Its respectable white and few black members, their sashes of mourning for lost freedom falling from their shoulders to the hems of their black skirts, would gather silently outside town halls. Their lugubrious presence shoved aside by police, they would disperse only to reassemble at the next corner to face the next charge, the next outburst of mockery from the passing citizenry. Afterwards they would go home, their names in police notebooks. They would sleep at night with the sounds of police boots in the shrubberies, flashlights stroking their bedroom windows, waiting to be woken at 2 a.m. to be asked questions about their friends, their children's friends.

Even in Cape Town, Mrs Raikes would be a centre of unease. The right-wing and fascist white women students would hiss and heckle in probably genuine disgust. The non-political women (if they could tear themselves away from their boyfriends to attend) would be embarrassed at the tales of women old enough to be their mothers being harassed by police the age of their sons, and doing nothing to defend themselves. The left-wing students, both black and white, would merely be scornful of an organization naive enough to think that wickedness could be shamed into any kind of self-awareness.

Sitting beside Mrs Raikes, Lilian would squirm under their stares, too aware of the message of her dark face beside Mrs Raikes's pale one. She, the thoroughly westernized descendant of an Indian clan grown rich on trading with poor Africans, who wore a sari only for weddings and religious festivals, who was occasionally invited into smart white houses, would attract a separate hostility. But that was her private problem.

For she hoped that, somehow, something of the stature of this woman who, herself so natural a figure of authority, had fought authority for twenty-five hard years, would convey itself to the students. This woman had not given up when other women had given up; she had selected for herself this limited and unglamorous part in the resistance. She would, expecting little of success and setting no great value on her role, continue to play it — all the way from imprisonment to enduring some tedious vicar's address at a fund-raising bazaar — until her death.

If love needed a reason to exist, this would be, in part, the reason Lilian loved Mrs Raikes. It was, however, also the reason she had not declared that love. In times of hot war, passions may rage. In the cold season of covert war, things are held in an icy reserve. Lilian's love was an irrelevance. It would be so until the day she would cut down those two policemen with a panga. This was a continent without emotion.

Yet there was, on this marathon run, some release. Driving fast on the empty dead-straight roads, they would spur the powerful engine, slice through the miles, telegraph poles whipping past their ears. When Lilian could capture Mrs Raikes's mood, some fun was to be had in outrunning the police car, a poor match for the powerful Bentley, its radiator now gasping for breath a quarter-mile behind them. Fun, but children's fun, make-believe. The air crackled with the radio waves of the real apparatus of the state. Until they irritated the two men behind enough to bring out the beast, the Toyota was a game, a memorandum on the drawing of limits bearing a postscript that they were not important enough to rate being shadowed by a helicopter.

Mrs Raikes reached out for the flask of whisky. 'You like driving, don't you? That's nice. It makes the car sing.'

Lilian started. How much more of her thoughts had Mrs Raikes been able to read?

'I'd like to ask you to do it again, but you'll have to start your own speaking tours soon — which you'll do extremely well of course, but what a waste of a superb chauffeur!'

Lilian flushed. 'They say people of my race make good servants.'

Mrs Raikes dropped her eyes. 'I'm sorry,' she said. Then, after a pause, 'I think I was trying to find out how far I could go — impertinent in itself, of course. But I won't be the last to do it. In politics, my dear, they peel away your privacies.'

'Oh, it's all right. I'm not offended. I'll drive you anytime.'

'Why?'

The words formed themselves in Lilian's mind; they moved to an inch from her tongue — Because I want to be with you. Because I think that you are strong and will be stronger with me. Because I want you. She said: 'Because it's worthwhile.'

'Are you sure? Nobody fears us; we have no guns; we won't change anything.'

'You changed me.'

'Perhaps you aren't important, my dear.'

Lilian bristled. 'I was born here. This is my country.'

'That's what the two men behind us would say. And what follows?'

'For them? That I'll kill them for killing my country.'

'Not change them?'

'You must be joking!'

'Then you're in the wrong organization.'

A swishing in the grass, out of tune with the wind, reminded Lilian that this was not a private conversation. Her companion, still leaning against the car, seemed not to mind. How could she, through all these years, bear it?

'But I hope you'll stay,' Mrs Raikes continued, 'At least for a while.'

'Maybe I will. I didn't join for the tea parties.'

'God no. Nor me,' said Mrs Raikes with feeling.

Lilian laughed. She laughed as she took a slug of whisky, her lips finding the fragrance of the mouth which had just released the flask more powerful than the unfamiliar fire inside. She laughed as the wind shifted the arthritic branches of the thorn tree to allow little streaks of sunlight to run across Mrs Raikes's form. She laughed with sheer joy at the open road, the vast sky, and the twenty-four hours alone on this road with the most wonderful woman in the world.

About the overnight stop in De Aar, she did not laugh. She was not even sure whether she feared it more than she longed for it. Certainly, she expected trouble from the police. More immediately, she feared that something inside herself might break free, tear down and destroy the easy fondness of women's friendship, the one small outlet for her flooded feelings, facilitated by the twenty-year gap in their ages, by Mrs Raikes's magnificent self-centredness, by the colour of Lilian's skin.

The little kettle screeched. As Lilian made the tea, Mrs Raikes detached herself from the body of the car and sat, cross-legged, in the grass nearby, finishing off the whisky. There was no milk, only one mug. Lilian seated herself opposite, putting the mug down between them.

'Be careful; you might scald the ants.' Mrs Raikes pointed to the little column of shiny red forms.

'Ouch. Those bite!'

'Not if you sit still.'

With difficulty, Lilian sat while half a dozen miniature monsters mounted her ankle and made towards the leg of her bermudas.

'Sometimes,' said Lilian thoughtfully, 'I think you are more of a Hindu than I am.'

'You flatter me.' Mrs Raikes leaned over and gently flicked the ants off Lilian's knee, nudging them again when they turned and challenged her finger with upraised pincers.

I could, thought Lilian, so easily kiss her now, right here under the lens of the Special Branch camera. I think she might not even be angry if I did. We wouldn't feel the ants, the police. She said: 'You deal gently with opponents, don't you?

'When they're small enough, my dear.'

'Those two men are small to you.'

'I want them to be. I like to win — an infrequent pleasure.'

Lilian knew that her naked stare in response to another of those wry smiles was telling what was surely already known; was asking, not for the first time, for a signal. Did she see something in the grey eyes?

But Mrs Raikes looked away. 'I'm very fond of you Lilian,' she said, too dryly. 'And I do approve of your joining the Sash — for one must do something though the big things will not be done by people like me — but I think it's only the start for you. I think you're going to get into trouble.'

'I'm not afraid.'

'No you aren't, are you? Soon you will become impatient with us. You have skill and discipline. You could be useful to the people who will do the big things — if you want to give your life to it.'

'Oh, I do.'

'Ask yourself that question in another twelve months,' said Mrs Raikes, with a sigh. 'You've only been with me for as many weeks, and I'm not ready to give you up yet. Tell me, why did you join?'

Lilian thought. It was different for Mrs Raikes who had come from Europe in the fifties, the bride of a mine magnate's son. At first sight, she had declared the society she saw around her disgusting. With the grand confidence of a metropolitan among colonials, she had discomforted Johannesburg's most elegant dinner parties. Then she had joined the Black Sash and received no further invitations to dinner parties. Her husband, who acknowledged the duty of the wives of wealthy men to devote themselves to good works or breeding dogs, had at first been tolerant and gone out into society alone. Later he went accompanied by his secretary, a pretty young woman, now his new wife.

But Lilian had been born in Johannesburg. She knew no other world. To her, the iron walls enclosing her community were natural structures, the people outside — black and white — different, brutal, frightening. Safety was a narrow path through marriage to a second cousin and staying rich enough to buy some small peace for the ghetto. What had changed this?

'Well', she said, 'I realized when I was in my late twenties that I was never going to start wanting to get married.'

'Sensible in itself, my dear, but hardly sufficient reason.'

'In a way it was the beginning. It was my first refusal to live in a continent without emotion. Then I had a piece of luck. Three African women joined Naidoo Brothers as clerks. They made friends with me. They went to a great deal of trouble; I was very jumpy at first. I hadn't known any Africans before. I hadn't met women who took it for granted that we were all just women. I mean, they never seemed to doubt that I, an Indian, could also catch cold, fall in love, covet a pair of shoes.'

'Yes.'

'They took me to a Sash meeting. My father insisted on providing an escort, my kid brother. He sat outside in the car. And I heard your Cape Town speech.'

'You liked it?'

'It made me start to think, start to feel — I realized that my whole body had been numb and cold — I came to life. You could say I liked it!'

'That's reassuring. I get rather bored with it.'

'Surely not.'

'It's my job. It gives me a tidy life. But sometimes I would like to get out of uniform.'

'You don't have to wear uniform with me!'

'With you more than most people. I am your general. You are my lieutenant.'

Lilian allowed her eyes to go naked again. 'Tonight, could I just be your friend?'

Mrs Raikes's face was vague. 'We don't know the schedule of our two friends in the culvert, my dear.' Then she rose stiffly to her feet; said, firmly, 'Well, it's two hundred miles to De Aar. If our friends are sufficiently rested, we ought to set off. Want to toss for which of us does the first hundred?'

Mrs Raikes lost. 'I'll do the first stint anyway,' said Lilian, who could tell by the way her companion was moving that her back still hurt.

It was a brutal two hundred miles: due west, straight into the needles of the lowering sun, the road intermittently shadowed by rows of koppies to the north, these shadows deepened almost to darkness by her sunglasses. The grey Toyota metamorphosed from challenge into threat. And in these conditions it would be horribly easy to mow down a young antelope darting to the other side for its evening grazing, or even a child herding a few goats or cows. Yet Lilian wanted to press out of the engine all the speed it could give, to bring De Aar closer: De Aar, good or bad, was fate.

De Aar was also, as Mrs Raikes remarked as they slowed down to enter the dusty main street shortly after nightfall, a place unlikely to be gentle with a Black Sash picket. A rickety cattle-marketing town gloomed by the floodlit edifice of the Dutch Reformed Church (itself partnered by a viciously-buttressed town hall), it offered travellers the choice of two hotels, each with its ground floor given over to a raucous bar. There seeming nothing to choose between them, as the Special Branch car hovered behind, they approached the one on the left-hand side of the road.

'I can't go in there,' said Lilian, pointing to a sign, bigger than the hotel's nameplate, over the door which read 'Net blankes — whites only'.

'Your money's white enough, my dear.'

'Well, I *won't* go in there.'

Mrs Raikes gestured towards the other hotel, similarly decorated. 'It get's cold at night, so close to the mountains. Want to sleep on the road?' Three white men, fighting drunk, emerged from the bar. 'And we'll need some protection from them and their brothers. Best to be above them, with a lock on our door.'

Lilian started: 'Our door?'

'It's safer to share; if you don't mind.'

Lilian shook her head. She didn't mind.

Wordlessly she followed her companion to the tobacco-stained desk, returning the stare of the receptionist while Mrs Raikes demanded the manager. That crisis resolved to Mrs Raikes's satisfaction, Lilian took up the pen after her and wrote NAIDOO, in huge block capitals; then she followed up the creaking stairs while Mrs Raikes and the coloured porter chatted about the timely arrival of the spring rains.

The room was large and very bare, decorated, as if in defiance of the recently-added squalid bathroom, only by a large white basin and ewer between the two sagging bedsteads. The unshaded light gave the white earthenware the gravity of a tombstone. The porter drew the curtains, shutting out the church, and switched on an electric bar fire which emitted a loud buzzing noise but little warmth. Not an intimate room.

As soon as the porter had left, Lilian leapt to turn to the wall a louring portrait of the State President with military decorations and spectacles.

'Those are gestures, my dear, which will do no good, and may embarrass the cleaners in the morning. They have to make some kind of life out of all this.'

'I don't care. I'm not having him glaring at me while I undress.'

'He'll be watching anyway. His spies aren't all in cars. You gave up what little you had of freedom when you joined even our meek organization of women.' Mrs Raikes kicked off her shoes and stretched her long body out on one of the beds. 'Oh well, my back's not going to enjoy this mattress. We ought to be thinking about supper, but right now I could do with a drink. How about you?' She lifted the clumsy black telephone.

Lilian wandered about the room uneasily. It was such a horrible room, a prison. It was all the things she most hated about white people's cold tastes. She had, insofar as she had allowed herself to envisage the night, imagined somewhere plain but uncorrupted, a place where it might be possible, once again, to take out a cigarette and put it between those severe but beautiful lips. Here? A roar rose from the bar down below. Here there was no more than a tunnel vision portrait of the woman once again stretched out on the bed. Lilian yielded to her familiar rage at the blankness of the world.

'Come sit by me, Lilian my dear. My eyes are too tired from the road to follow you round the room.'

Lilian sat. Yes, the steel-grey eyes were tired, the rays of lines beside them etched into dry skin.

Mrs Raikes smiled. 'We're still waiting,' she said, 'for our friends from the Toyota to knock at the door.'

Lilian started. 'Waiting. Is that what we're doing?' Her voice was suddenly angry. 'You spoke about supper; you ordered a drink. I thought there would be some time. You said they were "small" opponents, that you liked to win. I need to talk to you. Nothing is resolved. Why can't you tell me what's going on. I thought you said...'

'Let's try to wait, dear girl, as the young Mahatma Gandhi waited, perhaps often, in rooms like this one. We are part of a moment in history.'

'Don't patronize me. Gandhi belongs to my history, not yours. You let me think there was some time, some time for you and me. You let me think we were fighting, not just sitting prey. Tell me what's going on.'

'I don't know. I don't know what's going on. I know they hate us and I think I know why. We don't tell them they're the enemy: we tell them — speaking as women, as all women — we say that human beings can love one another. They don't know what to do with that information. It pains them.'

'I don't care about their damn pain. I only care about yours, and mine.' Lilian jumped up off the bed; sat down again. 'It'd relieve my pain to give them some,' she said, more quietly. 'If I had a knife in their guts, I could feel free!'

'It's organizations like ours, my dear, which enable a society to go through revolution and still remain civilized. Otherwise the knife you twist in their entrails will also twist in yours.'

'Perhaps I'm ready to take that on.' Perhaps, Lilian thought, this rage that comes out of love is more than love.

'I would not hate you for it.'

'No?'

'No. You would have to hate me. But maybe your children's children could love us both.'

Lilian's hands stilled. 'Love us?'

'If Africa's Gods give them a chance.' Mrs Raikes's tired eyes were fixed on Lilian's hands. 'Perhaps they might be giving us a chance now,' she said. 'Smooth my brow, dear girl, with your cool palms.'

The ugly room faded away as Lilian gently pushed back the damp grey curls and laid her hand on the beautiful head. Her eyes caught a look. With a sharp intake of breath she received the knowledge that her lips could follow to the place where her hand now lay.

'I love you,' she whispered in a voice so low even her own ears caught no sound.

'Don't say that. This country's Gods give lovers no favour.'

It came at that moment, the thumping at the door. The porter flung it open; his face was set with fear. 'Madam, the police are here, at the front door, at the back, at the windows. They want you.'

Mrs Raikes sat up. 'Thank you, I'll be down presently. Have you brought our drinks? Oh good.'

Very leisurely, Mrs Raikes handed Lilian a glass, and took a sip from her own. 'Oh well,' she said, 'This is what they usually do. I thought they might have had some new ideas.'

Lilian was now bolt upright, her hands throttling the glass. 'No, oh no,' she stammered. Then firmly, 'We'll fight.'

'Save that, my dear. This is nothing much. They'll just keep me in for questioning tonight. The hotel people won't throw you out: they haven't been paid yet. Try to get a good night's rest; I may ask you to do most of the driving tomorrow.'

Lilian flung her free arm around Mrs Raikes's shoulder, spilling whisky over the candlewick of the bedspread.

'Perhaps that may survive too, my dear, at least let's give it another chance. We'll try overnighting at Knysna on the way back.'

The porter saw Mrs Raikes out of the room and down the stairs, then returned. He removed the whisky-stained cover on Mrs Raikes's bed, folded down those on the other. He seemed not to find it strange, to be waiting on another black person.

'You will stay to look after that lady?'

Lilian nodded. 'For a while.' Then, 'But I will have to go away for my new work.'

'Shame.' He picked up the glasses. 'Why do they want her?'

'Because they got it wrong. It's me they should want.'

'Good luck.' He closed the door gently.

Since February 1990, many women's organizations in South Africa have disbanded to throw in their lot with the ANC Women's League. The Black Sash has retained its independent structure but works closely with the women in the ANC and other bodies.

Night at the Rana's Palace

A palace guard strokes the thick Indian night with his flashlight, drawing white arcs over grass and shrubbery, then up the outer walls to turrets where the monkeys sleep.

In the courtyard, it is as if the evening had never been. Chairs that squeaked and scraped beneath hot talk of art or politics are now stacked neatly under canvas. Sitars and drums, brilliant Rajasthan silks, tall glasses clinking with ice, playing cards shuffled at the speed of light, jokes, quarrels, advice on the best way to cook rogon josh, the couple kissing behind the rathcoranni tree — all gone.

Everything is quiet. Even the baby monkey, whose howl broke into the darkness of Heide's dream, has been silent since she pulled back the curtain.

Heide, standing now at the long window, the curtain half covering her nakedness, breathes deeply, slowly, letting the dream slip away, waiting for consciousness to possess and change what had seized her in her dream.

The dream began, accurately enough, in memory. The woman was dancing as she had danced down there in the courtyard, her red, green and gold sari now flying to keep up with her feet, now settling over the curve of a shoulder. Santoshni they said her name was: Santoshni, Asha's cousin.

The faithful Asha was there in the dream too, standing behind Heide's chair as she had in the courtyard. She was there when the dancer ran towards them making movements like flowing water with her arms, ran up so close Heide could feel the heat of her body.

Heide, slightly uncomfortable, stared at the bare feet with nails painted red, breathing easier when she felt Asha's soft touch on her sleeve. But only for a second. Because Santoshni's waving fingers drew back, formed, just in front of Heide's face, the hard shape of a heron's head, and stabbed at her throat. That touch, though light and momentary, left Heide's skin stinging, as if from a burn.

Up till then, everything that happened in the dream mirrored what had happened in the courtyard. What came after was best left unexamined; it was no more than fumes of the wine, heaviness of the night, the queer, unanchored feeling of lying alone in a bed. It was nothing to do with Santoshni. Santoshni is real. She is, like Asha, a minor relative of the Rana's, also welcome at his parties because she leads a life not approved by her parents.

Heide, her throat burning again, soothes it with her fingers. Perhaps Santoshni's life does encompass those other things (also not normally approved by parents) that Heide's dream had begun to make. But they mean nothing, are certainly not what Heide wants.

In any case, Heide is a little afraid of the real Santoshni (as she always is of bold, clever, self-absorbed women who display their beauty contemptuously, as if to a rabble behind bars.) Heide rather dislikes her in fact. She rather resents that so much of Santoshni's rudeness — to Heide, the Rana, but most of all with Asha — was allowed to pass for wit down there in the courtyard. But then all kinds of things are possible at the weekend parties of Rana Vikram Singh.

'I call them lived fantasies, my dear kittens,' the Rana had said to Asha and Heide as he led them in through the great carved doors and handed them over to a servant. 'Call them an escape from that loathsome institution, Indian democracy.'

Heide takes another slow breath, and lets it out into a night almost palpable with warmth and moisture. The guard is still prowling. He wears a scaled-down uniform now — no headdress fanned high as a cockatoo, no red, green and yellow sash weighted at the hip with a dagger, but still the oversized white spats and holster polished so bright that the leather outshines the pistol. Gone like her dream, the red, yellow, green, the colours of Rajasthan; in their place the silver, blue, black, the colours of the night.

How can this quiet follow such a dream? How could the noise, motion, falseness of the evening slow to this huge stillness? Perhaps, if Heide can calm the agitation inside her, she will find some meaning in the dream. Perhaps, if she breathes slow, she can become part of an Indian night that opens into a huge space, but puts nothing in it beyond a darkness thick with mist and no moon.

She will try to make some sense of being alone. Asha will not have heard the monkey; her room is in the other wing, looking out towards Jaipur. How odd it feels to have Asha's world all around her, but not Asha. Odd, but necessary, because at the Rana's parties all rooms are single rooms ('Although you may my dear kittens, if you wish, and whom you wish, visit.')

No doubt several of the guests, perhaps even some of the more important relatives, are now visiting; no doubt others, like Heide, stare at the night. So: shall she shake off the last of her dream and visit? Asha's door will not be locked. Asha, who has a proper respect for mosquitoes, will be asleep under the net, will stir and snuggle close when Heide slips in beside her. That thought brings a light skip of pulse in the stomach. Yes, she will visit.

But not yet. Heide wants more from this night. Now, looking down into the space, she wants a little while apart from Asha. Asha loves India — when she is at home in London with Heide, or failing that, in Calcutta or Madras, as far as possible from her vast and claustrophobic family. Asha doesn't want to be here at all: this weekend, the only palace she wanted to visit was the Palace of the Winds in Jaipur — to count the bullock carts on the street below and calculate how many of their cargoes would fit into one Sainsbury van.

Dear Asha, whose views on economics are so much more

alarming to the Rana than Santoshni's views on sex. In this quiet night, Heide reaches out for Asha, echoing her clasp at Asha's arm earlier this evening, her shock at Santoshni's little stab at her neck. Had this caused offence?

Because Santoshni whirled away on little twists of the feet while the drummer's tapping fingers accelerated into a roll, yielding to the sitar only when Santoshni flew down the steps and threw herself onto the grass.

Heide, breathless now as she was when it happened, stares out at the stretch of coarse Rajasthan grass, blue-black in the darkness, searching for the spot where Santoshni lay staring at the stars. Heide had barely dared look at her then, and yielded gratefully to Asha's comforting arm and her whisper: 'Don't take any notice of that stupid little tart.'

'But what does it mean, Asha? Why did she attack me?'

Asha just shrugged. 'Maybe she fancies you.'

The fabric of the curtains is lightly touching Heide's breasts, making them burn as Santoshni's fingers had burned her throat. 'Maybe she fancies me. Maybe that's why I dreamed about her,' Heide says into the night. Everything is odd. It is odd that Asha doesn't seem at all to mind another woman fancying her lover. Heide minded: she felt like prey.

In the dream she *was* prey, Santoshni, her sari billowing, descending on her like a hawk.

But none of this matters now. Now she is alone with the Indian night, she and the monkeys asleep in the turrets, clinging to the rim of this huge space. There is no connection between her and Santoshni, no wrong done to Asha, no cause for shame, nor for her breasts to burn. Heide will let them burn, let this feeling run through her body and out into the night, emptying itself into something far out from sensation, something without words. Like the monkeys, she will pour her breath into the thick, dark space.

But breath comes fast, too fast. 'Forget that awful dream now,' Heide says sharply to herself. 'It's not Santoshni you want, it's India.' And Santoshni is certainly not India. At this elegant if rather self-conscious party, she stood out not through her beauty (although she is beautiful) or because her dance was graceful (although it was), but because she brought discord everywhere she went.

Especially with them. When she came back up into the courtyard, her sari glued to her back with dew, she evaded the men closing in on her, to sit, cross-legged, at Heide's feet. 'Do you like my dancing?' Her voice, strongly accented, was deep, in the manner of well-born Indian women.

'Why, yes.' Heide turned to the sharp, dark-eyed face. Santoshni was staring at her, unsmiling, as if she expected Heide to say something important.

Heide stumbled: 'I hadn't seen Indian classical dance before.' Santoshni was still staring; Heide reached behind for Asha's hand. 'Asha had told me how sensual it is.'

Santoshni nodded slowly. 'She did? Well now you know that it's arch, coy, repetitive, boring; sensual only to convent girls like Asha.'

Asha interjected ' — In the view of ex-convent girls like Santoshni — '

' — who learned it watching Asha dance in a pathetic attempt to entice the Mother Superior — '

' — but at least didn't dance like a tart.'

They were snapping at each other, but Santoshni was still watching Heide.

'I danced' (Santoshni spoke directly to Heide) 'like a divine tart. While poor Asha, born with frog feet, had to partner the needlework mistress.'

To Heide's relief, the stout form of the Rana loomed. 'Kittens, kittens.' His hands reached out to two pairs of heaving shoulders.

'Thank you uncle.' Santoshni flicked his hand away. 'Now do something useful. My cousin hasn't danced. Lay on some disco sound so she can do what she does best, flop about like a stork.'

The Rana, at least, acknowledged Heide. 'These two haven't stopped quarrelling,' he said apologetically, 'since they were in kindergarten.'

Heide nodded. It was all right. But she felt uneasy. And Santoshni's eyes were still pinning her to the chair.

'And now my dear people,' the Rana turned to the more important relatives, drifting away to join their fellows playing bridge under the verandah, 'no more of family bickering. We shall have a little poetry. Who will be first to recite?'

Looking out into the night, Heide feels a return of the sudden heat to her cheeks. Asha, who fled the family for Europe, has more in common with Santoshni the rebel than any in the mass of relatives now swallowed up in marriage or the civil service. In their seven year partnership, Asha has talked often about aunts, second cousins, but scarcely mentioned Santoshni. Heide hadn't even known they were at school together. Their greeting earlier in the evening had been polite and formal. Was it surprising that she was taken aback by the sudden flash of conflict?

Did it come from some ancient rivalry? Had Santoshni, her urchin's face peeping cheekily between clouds of silky hair, always stolen friends from Asha, tall and gawky as a Kashmiri? And tonight? Did Santoshni's rude approaches to Asha's lover come out of some old habit of pillage?

'Good, then,' says Heide out into the night, 'that I was cold to her. And I'm glad I put her out.' But the dream hasn't yet dissipated, and Heide still feels odd, engaged but in some queer way left out. Asha ought to have warned her about Santoshni. Heide is at a disadvantage, in a strange country, surrounded by Asha's past and Asha's people, in need of guidance, security, occasionally being with someone who doesn't ask when she is going to get married — someone like Santoshni.

When Asha snapped at Santoshni, was it to warn her off? If so, it failed badly. Because Santoshni leapt to her feet at the Rana's call for a poetry recital. Standing only a few feet from Heide's chair, still staring straight at her, she said she had something particular to say to Heide, in a free translation from Bhartrhari:

> In the dreaming forest of her hair
> under mountains of her breasts so fair
> lustful tiger stalks the night —
> Beware.

'Excellent,' called the Rana, rather too enthusiastically. 'Seventh century Sanscrit, Bhartrhari, very classical, very classical indeed.' He turned to Heide: 'Would you care to follow, my dear? If you like' (there was a touch of appeal in his voice) 'with a few verses of our gentle Wordsworth.' But chairs scraped as the last of the more important relatives left to play bridge.

Santoshni was unrepentant. Returning to sit at Heide's feet, she said: 'Do what Uncle says, now give us something about daffodils. Dedicate it to Asha, to Asha's faithfulness; remind me that the fashion in the West is for monogamy these days.' Tilting her head slyly, she added: 'You see, in India, we are a little behind the times.'

Heide breathes fast at this recollection. 'No, no, Santoshni,' she mutters into the night. 'You are too fast for me. You scare me.'

Now Heide half regrets that she didn't summon the nerve to stand up and recite as much as she can remember about 'wandering, lonely as a cloud', because then the scene that followed would never have happened.

'At the very least,' Santoshni said, rising up on a knee and leaning close to Heide, 'you can whisper in my ear that you like my poem more than the family does.'

Heide pulled back. Santoshni was not a nice woman; she was embarrassing the Rana; she quarrelled with Asha. 'No, I don't like your poem,' she said. 'It objectifies women.'

'It what?' Santoshni's voice shrank. 'I don't know what "objectifies" means.'

Asha was delighted. Clapping Heide on the shoulder, she told Santoshni to 'take a trip to the West some time; get yourself deconstructed.'

'You know I can't travel like you,' said Santoshni quietly,

'You know I haven't got money for a ticket or qualifications for a job.'

Heide, tightening the curtain around her, draws another slow breath. That was when it happened. Now, staring into the night, she can see the mechanism at work. Santoshni, happy to trade insults with everybody else, could be wounded by one word from Heide. Now she wanted, just for a second, to meet the eyes that had been pouring into hers, to show she hadn't meant to hurt. But when she caught them, something inside her exploded. Heide, trying to remember what happened next, hopes she looked away quickly.

Out in the night, there is a small movement — a snake, a mongoose, a rockrabbit? The monkey may have seen that too, but not Asha, whose room faces the other way. Perhaps Santoshni saw it because — Heide lets out the information she has kept tucked away — two rooms to her right, tucked in beside the important room that forms the junction with the centre block, is Santoshni's little room.

Can it be that Santoshni also heard the monkey howl, and, sari flung aside, now stands at her window wearing the silver, blue and black of night on her skin?

Santoshni had made mock of the beautiful sari. Suddenly bursting out with: 'I suppose this thing "objectifies" women', she pulled the skirts up hard between her legs like a peasant weeding the kitchen garden, and ran off to frighten the more important relatives playing bridge. Santoshni is so transparent, so defenceless somehow.

If she is at the window now, what is she doing? Does she, when the guard is out of range (because in India one takes care to protect oneself from one's protectors), strike poses for the night? Does she do this for Heide, knowing, through some electricity of the Indian air, what she did in the dream? Does she know how close Heide's room is? Surely she knows all the arrangements, for Santoshni is a regular visitor to the palace.

Then why doesn't she come to Heide? What exactly did she mean, snapping when Asha said it was long past their bedtime: 'Her bedtime too? Must she take orders from you because you look like a half-starved conscript in the Hindu Kush? I thought the fashion in the West was for women who looked like women.' But Asha steered Heide away, leaving Santoshni alone with the last of the wine.

Heide, curtain still wrapped around her, notes how easy it would be to take a half step onto the miniature balcony, to glance at the next window but one.

But she doesn't. She looks out into the space before her, at the turreted palace walls, a glimmer in the dark. Beyond the walls, runs the road to Jaipur. Listening hard, she can hear something, perhaps the grind of iron-shod wheels, the creak of harness as carts carry vegetables and job seekers towards the morning market, only two or three hours away. India pulses with life. Heide wants to know that life. She was beginning to feel it; she wants to again. She wants to open this wanting, to let in not the tiger of Santoshni's poem, but the real forest, the real mountain. But does she hear a movement, perhaps from the window of Santoshni's room?

Quick and casual, holding the curtain about her, she steps onto the balcony, peeps quickly to her right then pulls back into the shadow. Santoshni's room is in darkness, the curtains demurely drawn.

She must be asleep; hasn't heard the monkey, hasn't felt Heide's dream. Doesn't know that Heide's very bones melted when her sari, stretched wide as the wings of a hawk, hung in the air above Heide's bed, just for a second, before her body, still sweaty from the dance, fell hard.

Furiously, Heide pushes the curtain aside, and fumbles about the bed for the gown that had lain, folded with a snowy towel and ball of sandalwood soap, at its foot. She drags it on, and dashes into a corridor quiet as if patrolled by the palace guards.

She stops two doors down, not quite sure now that this is the right one. Shall she knock? Shall she turn the knob and peep quickly inside? She listens at the keyhole. It is very quiet, not even a whisper of carts on the road.

A door opens behind her, and a stout figure sidles out,

passes her close. The Rana, in a dressing gown, nods politely. 'Happy hunting, kitten.' Dangling from his hand is a musical instrument, a small lute. He makes his way towards the princely quarters on the second floor.

Heide finds herself giggling. This is absurd. The Rana is absurd, a pampered pet of the Indian democracy he despises. Heide is absurd: Asha is her life, her anchor. Santoshni is a half-hour's dream. If she lost Asha, she would have nothing to live for, or by. So? The other wing is not a thousand miles away. Marching bravely now, she heads down the corridor, past the important doors on the centre block, to the far wing and Asha's room.

It is closer than she remembered. She opens the door: a fresh, moist breath; the window is wide. She will fall on Asha as Santoshni fell on her in the dream. Hardly pausing, she parts the mosquito net: a head, high on the pillows, long wavy black hair, bright eyes staring at her.

A deep, well-bred Indian voice says: 'Hello. You've stepped into my dream. It was all about you.'

Heide is all confusion. 'Santoshni! Sorry, I'm sorry.' (No, wrong approach; think again) 'I thought this was Asha's room.'

'Asha? You want Asha?' Now Santoshni is smiling.

'Yes, well no, well, you see I was wakened by a monkey, I think it was a baby monkey — '

'You want a baby monkey?' And Santoshni pushes the sheet down past her breasts, spread wide, her little stomach, sunk between the bones of her pelvis, her open thighs. Between them lies a body; the dark, cropped head of Asha buries itself between Santoshni's pale legs.

'I'd so love it' — there is a smile in Santoshni's voice — 'if you'd join us.'

Heide is back in her own room, clinging to the cold iron of the balcony. Now the noises of the night are bursting her ears: the stamping of the guard, his flashlight flaming the shrubbery;

the groan of bullock carts dragging the desperate jobless to market; the thickening screams of parrots and monkeys as the first rays of dawn bring them back to hollow stomachs.

Soon, too soon, the door opens. Asha comes in. 'Remember I didn't want to come to this party.'

'I remember.' Later, or perhaps never, Heide will tell that she too was Santoshni's midnight lover.

The Rana is back in the princely quarters, and they are throwing things into suitcases like strangers after a one night stand, avoiding each other's eyes. At breakfast they will excuse themselves from the polo game, head for Jaipur, Delhi and then a place, that seems to belong to some long forgotten dream, called home.

Jonquil

I want to remember Jonquil, my friend of four hours. Though I did not write. Now I don't suppose I can, even if her scrawl over half a page of my address book were legible. But I want to remember her.

It happened on a Bee-Wee flight to Jamaica, a luxurious flight because the seat next to me — like most of the seats in the tail — was empty. (The non-smoking section was, of course, crammed to the gills.) I had stuffed the papers for my meetings into the seat pocket and was launched into Anita Brookner's chilly-hearted *Hotel du Lac*: Edith observing her fellow hotel guests from a fastidious distance.

In the same spirit I glanced around at my companions. There were four in view: two white men with their plump, pink arms bulging out of Hawaiian shirts; directly in front and on chatting terms with them were a black man and woman, also young, one a Rasta skinny as a Javanese puppet, the other had a Grace Jones haircut. They were smoking, whispering, swinging round, laughing — likely to be irritating after the first round of drinks. There was nothing else to look at.

I resumed communication with Brookner. Her hero Edith was now awkwardly circling two women, the start of a heartless hotel friendship, that poor palliative against loneliness. I faced sixteen days in hotels full of important gentlemen at conferences with whom I would not try to start friendships. During those days I would talk to my lover on the telephone, revelling in her warm, husky, 4 a.m. voice, but otherwise my heart would be always strapped into uniform. It would leap at the sight of the Blue Mountains or the 12-feet tall canna lilies, but not very high, because for me there is no real pleasure alone. At the meetings, it would quicken only at the chance to contradict the chairman. Later it might envy the men and women from a dozen countries sizing each other up; but for me there would be no couplings.

The woman with the Grace Jones haircut was passing on her way to the lavatory. She wore a khaki jump suit, like a giant baby's romper; it looked well on her strong frame. I took in the stiletto-heeled sandals, on which she walked with surprising ease, and noted that one of the loutish white men followed close behind her — too close, crowding close. She didn't seem bothered, but I was.

And that, I suppose, gave the lead. When she returned, still shadowed by the Hawaiian shirt, I shut Brookner up in midsentence and watched. He slipped into his seat behind and she bounced into hers, craning over the back to talk to him. She was perhaps 25 years old, pretty as a satyr with her round, dancing eyes and cherry mouth. She was talking about food, offering to trade her starter for anybody's spare pudding, wondering, arching her delicate brows, if she might get three beers at once when the trolly came round — rattling on about nothing at all. Not intimate, but not at all bothered.

The Rasta man beside her had begun to sing. Over the sound of the plane — that monotonous drone that seems after a while to be inside one's body, supplanting its heartbeat — I became conscious of a voice, a light bass, singing Bob Marley songs. She chatted in counterpoint. The two white men, hidden now in their seats, were inaudible. Then the Rasta, breaking into a piercing countertenor, began to sing 'Lord Rendell', that sinister tale of betrayal and revenge. I had not before noticed how alike they were, reggae and medieval ballads, music breaking out of pain.

> 'I've been to my sweetheart Mother;
> Make my bed soon, for I'm sick to my heart,
> And I fain would lie down.'

The drinks trolley cut them off for an interminable discussion over orderings. I don't think she got her three beers. The Rasta interrupted his song just long enough to ask for a coke. When the view cleared, I saw her back up over the seat again, begging the two men behind, from whom little wisps of smoke arose, for cigarettes. Then asking again, petulantly. Then she looked my way. I nodded, and handed her mine.

'Gee, thanks a trillion.' Now I was sure of the accent: Jamaican. But the diction wasn't. She must have seen lots of old American films; perhaps she had lived in the States. Perhaps she just liked disguises. She had a history. But she had no further use for me or the two men behind, and settled down. The plangent singing continued. I returned to the hotel by a lake, where a lonely woman, her cardigan buttoned against the Alpine winds, observed other exiles. The meal came, shutting off the singing. Was it lunch, was it dinner? It was 5 p.m. in London, noon in Kingston; wherever we were it was sometime sharp and sunny. I looked up again at the four exiles; I would have liked to give the girl my apple charlotte.

Especially now that it was clear that she was aware of my watching; she was peering about, showing off a little, an awkward kind of flirting aimed, I judged with pleasure, not at the two white men but at me. I pondered a move casual enough to lead her on without giving an opening for a snub. Her glance swept past me and again, collecting information. In the next swing, I caught it, holding for a second the dancing eyes. Then she was back up on the seat, laughing with the two men. Perhaps she was joking about me. Fiercely, I whipped out the Brookner, spreading its pages over the remains of my meal.

Edith was now allowing herself to be tempted by the two bourgeoises to share their measured explorations of cream teas and Swiss dress fabrics. Why did Edith bother when all she sought from them was nourishment for her contempt? And why did this irritate me? If the girl with the Grace Jones haircut were less pretty, wouldn't I be studying her table manners in the same spirit?

'Howdy; is that seat empty?' The girl was beside me, gesturing at the window. 'Mind if I look out for Bermuda?'

I got up to let her in.

'I'm Jonquil. Headed for Kingston. I'm starving. Are you leaving your sweet?' Then, after apple charlotte, biscuits, cheese and bread roll, 'You had some fags?' Then, 'Gee whizz, it'll be good to feel the sun on my back.'

'How long is it since you felt the sun, Jonquil?'

'Six months and five days.'

That was a very precise measure. 'Were you six months and five days in England?'

'Yup.'

'Was it your first trip abroad?'

She nodded. 'Also my last. Anyway, reckon I got something out of it: this jump suit and twelve pounds; and I got wised up.'

She was a strange girl. Her eyes, wide in puzzlement at the world, constantly sought my gaze. Her soft Jamaican drawl slid over her speech, as if reluctant to release the words. A bouncy girl, but shy. A country girl. Yet each time she stubbed out a cigarette, she reached straight into my bag for another, having put the packs I gave her from my duty frees into her pocket.

'There's one heck of a lot of sea down there,' she continued. 'Maybe that's Bermuda, those cute white flecks. D'ya reckon we'll maybe overshoot Jamaica same way, so's I can forget thinking?'

'Why? Don't you want to go home, see your friends, your family?'

'Friends? I ain't got no friends. I got folks. They wrote me they'd be at the airport, but didn't say what they'd be there for.' Her eyes, close up to me, were big and serious, focused somewhere behind. 'Maybe to say goodbye. You see,' she said thoughtfully, 'we don't live in the same world no more.'

I was uncomfortable. She was too serious. She was pressing me too close. In my world, a seduction is accompanied by a little light banter, and a certain reserve. Also troublesome was the man who had followed her to the lavatory, now swiveled round staring at her with the same crowding air. Something was going on, something in which I was not included. But for all that, I had made a play for her attention, and got it, and it was me she was now sitting with. I returned his stare to let him know that I was not cowed by all this mystery.

'Oh, no bother about him,' she said. 'He's okay. He's just dropping me off at Kingston. I'm worth a free trip to the Caribbean to him. But he hasn't got my passport. Pilot's got that;

mine and the other guy's, the one that sings those mournful cowboy songs.'

Their passports held? A suspicion flickered in my head. I fished. 'Is he scared to go home, too?'

'Sure; he's got nowhere to go home to. He'll go someplace in the bush, I guess, and grow ganja again.'

So that was it! If I was shocked — I am, after all, a respectable, middle-aged lesbian — the only shock I recognized was from the gaze of those mild, puppy's eyes. Oh Jonquil, I thought, what are you? Have you done something really stupid, and have you such a child's sense of history that you think every day gives a new Jonquil?

She was waiting for a response. I was nervous. I wanted to back off a little. I asked her about the jump suit. She got it, she told me, from one of the other girls, in exchange for services. No problem. After that, she'd washed it, and pressed it under her mattress, to have it nice to wear home.

I asked her about her parents. They were good, decent folk, who had been pleased for her when she'd saved cash to go to the Mother Country, and a letter saying that she had a job back home and wouldn't outstay her welcome. They didn't question any more than she did the packages which good kind Uncle Gregory, who had helped pad out her savings, had asked her, casually, after she'd already made most of her arrangements, to take to his friend in Bethnal Green. After all, she hadn't much luggage to fill the metal trunk Uncle Gregory had loaned her; she was planning to buy lots of English woollies with the cash she would earn working nights in Gregory's friend's restaurant.

'I guess I thought, you see,' she said, 'that something would have to be all right if it was to go somewhere like Bethnal Green; I mean, it's not Brixton!'

She didn't see Bethnal Green. She didn't see Brixton either for that matter, nor Piccadilly Circus, nor Madam Tussauds, nor Oxford Street. At Heathrow, she was motioned aside by a pair of uniformed men with dogs, and what she saw of England was, through a grille in the back of a van, the Hammersmith Flyover and the traffic jam at the turn-off to Holloway Prison.

She couldn't well remember the trial. The place was so huge, and there was a jury — she tried to recall whether the jury, or only the judge and counsel wore wigs — and she was always being moved by big white men, to wait down here in this cell, to go up there to wait again in the corridor, to appear briefly in the mahogany room that smelled of men's hair-oil, to say 'not guilty' as she had been told to say, to go down again to the cell, to go up and wait outside with the men, to go in hear the judgment, to be marched out again and into the van and back to Holloway.

She had been frightened, she told me, but of the wrong things. She'd jumped at the long booming echoes that rolled through the court as if the roof was caving in. She was afraid that the Bible she laid her hand on might have been jinxed. She'd been scared of a man grinding his teeth in the courtroom, but he turned out to be the clerk. When the whole thing began to take rather a long time, she was afraid she'd been forgotten in the basement cell.

'I didn't know anything,' she said, with another of her baby's smiles. 'The girls at Holloway said I was a proper fanny and ought'a straighten up. Anyway, they told me I was lucky. They said twelve months was pretty good for a drugs charge and if I kept my head down, I'd be out in six. But at first, I didn't want to be out at all. I kept thinking this thing I got to do and thinking it would be better if I made myself die.'

My hand, instructed by the same urge which would cause it to restrain a child rushing out into traffic, grasped her arm: but this was not a child; and my feelings were not purely about her safety. I pulled back.

So did she. 'You white people give yourselves a lot of airs,' she said soberly; 'But that's okay; I know you like me.'

'I don't understand you,' I said uncertainly.

I meant, I suppose, that I didn't understand why, if she was going to tell me something so momentous, that she had let the information dribble out, inconsequentially, like a child's tale of its day at school. And her none-too-subtle advances; I couldn't get their measure: surely that arm, that foot, those eyes were not just payment for a few cigarettes? 'I don't understand,' I added, 'why you aren't angry.'

'Angry?'

'Yes.' She had left on her pilgrimage to the 'Mother Country', and been received as a criminal. 'Aren't you angry with England?'

'I guess,' she drawled, 'I wouldn't have liked it anyway. It's not like they tell you at school; its cold and greasy and full of white trash.'

'Surely you must be angry with Uncle Gregory?'

'What's the use in being angry?' she smiled softly. 'Better to make sure he doesn't do what he done to me to anyone else.'

I was impressed. I reflected on anger: perhaps, like the survivors of Nazi concentration camps who talked of their shame, grief and horror but not of anger, she was beyond that proud, perhaps facile, response to injustice. I made an effort to quell the anger I felt on her behalf. 'I'm really truly sorry, Jonquil,' I said, 'you had such a bad time.'

'Oh, it was all right. Not at first, when I couldn't talk to anybody, but after. The video was good. Lots of old Hollywood films. One of the girls — a white girl, old, but not so old as you, maybe thirty; she was in for soliciting — she wanted me to hide someplace and wait for her in England. But I knew that wasn't any use. I had to go back. 'Course I said I'd stay, but I threw away the address she gave me.' Another big, innocent smile. 'She was my protector, you see,' she continued, 'so I had to hide the jump suit from her. That's how I kept it till now. You like it, don't you?'

Yes, I did. I liked it a lot. I liked the feel of its silky cotton pressed against my arm, the way it bunched lightly at the crotch, then tautly wrapped Jonquil's long, athletic thighs. I liked the little open zips at the ankles, freeing a beautifully-shaped stilettoed foot to knock lightly against my shoes. I liked the sense of being played with by this innocent-knowing young woman who had smoked a dozen of my cigarettes in a couple of hours and was surely making me some kind of offer.

What offer? To be the successor of the other older white woman in for soliciting? She had parents waiting to say goodbye to her at Kingston. Would there be another trial which would leave her as homeless as the Rasta man? Did she want refuge with me at my hotel? Would she then hide the jump suit from me, while I tried to hide her from the chambermaids? Did I, a closet lesbian with a lover and a career, need a whole heap of new problems? Did I trust her?

Time to think. The trolley passed, and I bought her three cans of Red Stripe. We would soon be down for a pick-up at Nassau, when the prison officer in the Hawaiian shirt would again take her into custody. The Rasta was still singing:

> 'What have you been eating,
> Rendell my son;
> What have you been eating, my pretty one?'
>   'Eels and eel-broth, Mother;
> Make my bed soon, for I'm sick to my heart,
> And I fain would lie down.'

Did I want to trust her? Could I even think of trust when, though I had left my bag open for a pretty girl lacking any sense of property to take worthless things like cigarettes, I had carried it with me when I went to the lavatory? It would be trust to give her the power to disgrace me at conferences glossy with important gentlemen; but that would only be a part of it. I couldn't get away from the feeling that I would be taking far more of trust than I was giving, that she was so much the more vulnerable.

Lesbian is vulnerable. Woman is vulnerable. Young is vulnerable. Innocent is vulnerable. There was something else too: the only power Jonquil had exerted over a white woman had been sexual, a power she was now using on me. And Jonquil's people had been abused by my people for four hundred years of the most brutal slave order in the Western Hemisphere. I had loved black women before, but they had been older, educated, confident, had had more than twelve pounds—they were women you squared up to, who squared up to you. Jonquil was different. For any scene played out between her and me, the script had been written long ago, and my role was that of wolf. But my foot was burning from the touch of her foot and I wanted to try to take the moment, just for itself, as something with no past and no future, outside of history.

'Yes, I do like it. It's a very well cut jump suit,' I said.

She was sharp. 'No need to be so patronizing.'

I wanted to explain that, like Edith now warming very slightly to the overtures of the two bourgeoises, I was, in my way, flirting. But carefully, because between Jonquil and me was so little space we could make our own. I said: 'I meant to say how good it looks on you. Does it come from Next?'

'God knows. Fell off the back of a lorry into Holloway Prison.' Then, with bitter sarcasm: 'Jailbird gear, nice eh? Anyway, you was reading.'

I lunged at this little escape. 'Its a story,' I said, hastily, 'about a woman — a romantic writer — whose romantic life was being written for her by her friends, and she wouldn't play, so they sent her to a lonely hotel by a lake.'

'She should've told her friends to get knotted.'

'You're absolutely right, Jonquil.' Why hadn't I seen that? 'That's her problem; she doesn't.'

'It's lots'a people's problem, no big deal. I kinda felt something funny about Uncle Gregory's packages, but I didn't say.'

'No,' I replied thoughtfully. The Rasta's Lord Rendell, too, knew the eels his sweetheart gave him were the wrong colour, but he ate them.

'Then why don't you tell?' Her face was inches from mine.

'Tell what?'

'Tell me. Tell me to get knotted, or the other.'

I prevaricated. 'I don't know you.'

'No, you don't know the big thing. What I'm going to do with the twelve pounds.' She was whispering. 'Anyway, you couldn't stop me. You see, I'm going to spend five pounds of it buying some scent for my mother in the duty free shop at Nassau.'

'That's nice.' Another switch; she was an eel herself. Now she had me worrying there might be nothing to be bought in the Bahamas for a mere five pounds.

'But you know enough to say you fancy me.'

I jumped. I had given so much away? So what. It was just for the flight, outside of history. I laughed. 'But why should I do that,' I said lightly, 'unless you give me grounds to think there's a reasonable chance that you also fancy me?'

'Oh that. I don't.'

I choked on my laugh.

'No,' she continued, reaching into my bag for another cigarette, 'I don't fancy you at all. Not at all. Anyway, there's someone else always on my mind.'

'I see.' Coldly, I opened the book again, trying to focus on print jumping up and down in front of my eyes, on the problems of a woman who was too wet to tell her friends to get knotted; trying to cut out the sting of being led on to rejection by a pretty girl who was cleverer than Edith at playing power games with people she cared nothing for; cleverer than me at airplane flirtations outside of history. 'I see. I hope it goes well for you both.'

'Yup, I got it all planned. The other seven pounds is for him. I've thought about it night and day. I'm getting something very special for him. I know where it was in the hardware shop near the Kingston harbourfront just before I left.'

'The price will have gone up,' I said icily.

'I've allowed for that. It was eighty dollars Jamaican before, around a fiver sterling.'

'It will have been sold.'

'They'll have another.'

'Well, that's that then.' I wanted her to go away, stop blowing smoke into my face, pressing her arm right into my seat space, get lost. I wanted a few minutes by myself — time to rise to the bitter sense of the appropriate that my pack of fantasies had, as usual, dealt me the joker. So, Jonquil had a whole big world in which I had no place. So had the Rasta of the beautiful voice, and between him and me had been no connection for me to foul up. I turned away, to the singing.

> 'What will you leave your sweetheart?
> Rendell my son?
> What will you leave your sweetheat, my pretty one?'

Jonquil grasped my arm with irritation. 'I'll have to go with the Rastas after, and learn how to do that darn crooning. They're not proud like you, you know.'

'After what?'

'After I've been to the hardware store and got my present and used it, the knife to kill Uncle Gregory with.'

'Oh Jonquil, no!' My hand was again on an arm silky with muscle under the fabric of a well-made jump suit. My eyes met a solemn, child's stare.'No. Not that.'

'It's all fixed up. I'm gonna get him in his bed in his smart house on Hope Road. Tonight.'

'No, wait a bit. Listen.' — Oh, God, I thought, here goes, swallow the bait — 'I'm staying at the Terra Nova Hotel, room 21. Come there with me, and I'll help you get justice. I'll find you a lawyer.'

'Like the lawyer they gave me in London, so busy trying to feel my ass he couldn't get ahold of the charge? That's justice?'

> 'What will you leave your sweetheart, my pretty one?'
>   'A rope to hang her, Mother;
> Make my bed soon, for I'm sick to my heart,
> And I fain would lie down.'

Did I believe this? Did I need to believe any of her story? It touched my life at no point and I had no way to judge it. But I believed her. I believed her as easily as I believed Lord Rendell's rope and disbelieved Edith's passion for the man offstage in London — for, despite all of life and literature, I still can't quite shake off the feeling that heterosexual women are bluffing. We believe what we want to believe.

Jonquil got off at Nassau, trailed by the Hawaiian shirt, and came back with Yardley's Old English Lavender, which she several times wrapped and unwrapped as we inched towards Jamaica. At Norman Manley Airport, long after I had collected my luggage and lost sight of a battered metal trunk bumping round and round the carousel, she and the Rasta were still sitting quietly at the edge of the hall, waiting for the pilot to return their passports. Outside, as I searched the pack of taxi drivers for an honest face, I noticed a couple waiting: a woman with deeply furrowed brows, a man in white overalls, feet drumming against the washed stone floor. I wanted to go up to them, to say that Jonquil was all right; that Jonquil was not all right; that they should lay aside their grief and embrace her, because Jonquil might not be with them for very long.

But this was not my world. I belonged to the meetings and the cold alpine winds where Edith was now being courted by an Uncle Gregory in a suit of the palest grey.

Jo-Soap's Last Gift

The man was shaking a slip of paper. White as his coat when dipped into the liquid, it had come out stained green.

'It's as I thought, Miss Stokoe,' he said.

Miss Stokoe stroked the cat with a vague hand. 'Yes?'

'This colour' — he pointed — 'shows urea in the blood. Kidneys packing up now.'

'That's why she's stopped eating?'

'I'm afraid so.'

'I see.' The cat, a scruffy white moggy with round yellow eyes, slid its skinny frame between Miss Stokoe's arms and right into the shapeless tweed coat, worn even now in June. Molelike, it burrowed up between the bulges which marked the perimeter of Miss Stokoe's near-spherical tiny form until a head emerged at the collar. Miss Stokoe butted her chin against the cat's, then turned away against the ammonia on its breath. 'You can help her? I don't want to keep her alive artificially.'

'Quite.' The vet looked uncertain. 'Well,' he added, 'I could give Jo-soap a jab to slow her metabolism a bit, you know; she might respond for a while... .' He prepared the injection. Miss Stokoe offered the cat. The little bag of its body was visibly swelled by the five or ten millilitres of chemicals.

As the needle withdrew, Betty, the surgery assistant since the year dot, dabbed the bloody spot on the cat's rump with surgical spirit. Out of habit, out of that impulse towards tidiness that informed many things they did in the surgery, Betty murdered a million microbes. Not that this was a killing for any gain since kidney failure would beat any little local infection to the toss. Betty reckoned on two or three more dismal days. The cat, objecting to the swab more than the needle, crawled back inside Miss Stokoe's coat and let out a loud burring purr — the purr, well known to Betty, of cat fear. This was accompanied by a doubling of the smell of decay, the foretaste of death — also well known to Betty. She watched the vet, one of a succession of pimply New Zealanders, reach out a hand adorned with scratches to stroke the cat's half-buried skinny bum.

'We'll do all we can, Miss Stokoe,' he said. 'She has a strong heart. She might respond for a while. But you recognize that Jo-soap is old and not at all well.'

'I don't want to do anything that isn't natural,' repeated the foolish old woman. Her eyes, what you could see of them behind the pebble glasses, were blinking in some sort of smile.

'We have, um, a lot of kittens,' muttered the youth, 'in need of homes. We could get you one in, say, a week.'

'Oh no, thank you, oh no. Not at our age, not a kitten. And Jo-soap and I, you know, have been through so much together that a kitten would never be part of.' The cat changed gear to a soft, though still rather bronchitic, purr.

'Sometimes,' the vet persevered in that grinding way colonials do, 'we find that an old cat responds well to a kitten, a gentle one; gives them something outside of themselves to get interested in.' The man was a dolt. Jo-soap was well beyond that stage, locked now into her illness. Miss Stokoe, too, was past that; she would only worry about what would happen to the kitten afterwards. He was dragging out a torture which would be quite long enough. There was no future, for either of them. Jo-soap was dying. Miss Stokoe would soon follow. All this was pointless.

Anyway, it was now half an hour past clocking off time; it was time for Miss Stokoe to take her cat back to whatever cat-stinking hole she lived in, time for the vet to pick up whatever peroxide blonde he spent his evenings with; time for Betty to go home to do the washing up for Mother. And the bill. What was stopping the sentimental youth from getting the five pounds which would allow Betty to cash up and go?

'How did she get that unusual name, Miss Stokoe?' The vet's blonde had stood him up that evening it would seem.

The old woman's eyes twitched. 'It's years,' she said, 'since anyone asked that, isn't it, Jo-soap?' The cat's bottom disappeared and its head emerged again from the neck of the coat; again its mouth butted the hairy chin of the old woman. Betty turned away from this scene of intimacy and began to rattle instruments in the sterilizing chamber. But Miss Stokoe was now unstoppable. 'You see, it was actually a name for me,' she said almost gaily. 'It was what Jo made of me. One of my pupils — that was just before I retired — found her in a coal shed and brought her to school. She was starving you know, almost as thin as she is now. I took her home. I thought she was a kitten, but she was a teenager, and expecting.'

'Kittens?'

Betty snorted over the boiling water. Did the boy think she was expecting puppies?

'Four, my dear, hardly as big as mice. And she didn't have much milk so we had to hand-feed them. Then the problem of finding them homes.' Betty well remembered that little drama. Miss Stokoe had spent a fortune at the surgery on keeping the four runts alive and then spent another fortune advertising to get rid of them. Miss Stokoe's spectacles glittered under the lamp. She had obviously taken a shine to this New Zealander; Betty had never known her so chatty. Nor was she through.

'The poor mite wasn't housetrained, you know, and she stole everything in the kitchen. My dear friend Ellen — she's dead now my Ellen — said only a Joe Soap* would have taken in such a cat. So the laugh was on me.'

'Yes,' said the vet absently, clearly understanding the joke no better than Betty did.

'But it worked out. Ellen said later that it was because I was a Joe Soap that our Jo learned to see the funny side of things. At first, you see, poor Jo scratched me every time I stroked her. She

---

* *Joe Soap, a sucker; someone who allows everybody to take advantage of him; originally, I think, a music hall character*

didn't even know how to play.' Betty started at that strange remark. She looked back from the sterilizer. The cat's ears were twining in Miss Stokoe's greasy grey hair. That was play?

'Jo-soap is a fortunate cat.' (The vet must have learned truthfulness from a second-hand car salesman; what could be fortunate about death by inches?) 'Best bring her back tomorrow, and we'll see if she's making any progress.'

Betty lunged at the basket and held it open. Jo-soap recognized the cue and put herself into it, settling, like a discarded cardigan, a ruffled white lump at the bottom. Betty laced her down, tight. A moment of satisfaction. One day's work over. Tomorrow what? Innoculations for a parade of pedigreed brats grown fat on the canned remains of more chemically-swollen pedigreed flesh. More of the same. Some animals you killed and ate. Some animals you kissed and kept alive long after they would be worth eating. Some humans you kissed. Some humans you ate. Most humans, if you had any sense, you kept clear of. Then Betty did an idiotic thing. All that emotion swilling round the surgery; it must have been catching.

'I live quite near Valley Road,' she heard herself utter while the vet was breaking into a stupid grin. 'I'll lift you home.'

'You're sure it's not too much trouble?'

That's how you could get yourself caught, even someone like Betty who knew this world, and knew it for a sham.

Miss Stokoe was a little afraid of the surgery assistant, that tall, sergeant-major of a woman who scarcely moved her lips, never looked at one, whom nobody called by name. Yet, with her schoolteacher's experience of systems, Miss Stokoe knew that the surgery was a good one because Betty was its real manager. Many a time Miss Stokoe had seen Betty hand the necessary drug or instrument to a puzzled young vet. It was Betty who had brought under control the hysterical alsatian terrorising the waiting room; Betty who would instantly spot a real emergency and overturn, without a murmur, the appointments system she had invented and then built up to the status of Holy Writ.

Miss Stokoe hadn't always seen it like that. The first time she brought Jo-soap in, Betty had lifted out the flea-ridden kitten with fingers like tongs. Miss Stokoe thought she had offended her; she felt ashamed for herself and her kitten. Soon she realized that Betty was steely with everybody — and with vets she was savage. Later she became aware that Betty's coldness did not include that commonplace impatience with old people — impatience usually laced with hearty bonhomie — which she was learning, with difficulty, not to mind.

Indeed, if Miss Stokoe asked herself why she kept faithful to this practice in spite of anonymous vets and two buses to get to it, she would have to say that it was for the services of a woman she trusted but couldn't say she liked. Certainly a woman from whom one would not beg a favour — nor expect to be offered one. So the lift was almost a shock. It signalled for Miss Stokoe some solemn compassion of the sort one might get on the day of a funeral.

Miss Stokoe followed her orders and crawled into the back seat; the basket was dumped beside her. Jo, who hadn't travelled in a car since Ellen died, crouched quietly — too quietly. Miss Stokoe fingered the weave of the cane. Had Jo-soap taken in the sense of the vet's soft words, Betty's more speaking look as she lifted her onto the surgery table for inspection? Animals understood more than one knew. Yes, Jo-soap had surely understood the diagnonis, yet, when she had clung to her mistress, had done it not out of fear but in ordinary everyday fondness. Jo-soap reminded one that the revelation of a truth was an event only in the mind. Death itself was exactly as near or as far as it had been before; nothing had changed. For a moment, almost a moment of play, they had shared with a nice young man what they daily shared with each other: that it was just a wait. A short wait for Jo, an as yet undetermined wait for herself. At its own pace, death would go round the house, from room to room, and put out the lights.

Death, so momentous yet concealing from all except the dying its meaning, had taken Ellen almost casually. In the evening its only hint was an attack of indigestion — and then in the night, Ellen had sat up sharply, and rolled over, breaking with the soft groan Miss Stokoe knew so well from that other giving up of the ghost. Miss Stokoe had been been denied an illness which she could serve in a perfect act of love. Against this loss Jo was offering her own small recompense, going so far even to give Miss Stokoe the knowledge that she, not Jo, would determine the moment of this death. Reading Betty's look, Miss Stokoe believed this would be within a few days. It didn't matter. Life was sweet, painful and short. The terrors that invaded the night yielded, in the morning, to Jo's soft muzzle demanding love. Just as, so long ago, dreadful dreams had dissolved to nothing in Ellen's arms — Ellen who had been half the lights in Miss Stokoe's life. Just as, now, the figure in the driving seat could become for a moment of play a light driving out the darkness in her mind.

Betty drove fast, roaring past John Lewis's, round buses stopped for fares, up the hill. Miss Stokoe quickened a little with excitement. When they were brought up short by traffic lights, Betty's fingers tapped a military rhythm on the wheel. Perhaps that handsome woman ought to have been a soldier, a drill sergeant, an engineer building a pontoon to ferry troops across a swollen river. Betty didn't talk at all, nor look round. Her brows, the brows of a general pouring over a map, were furrowed. Betty, whose hard, lean form defied all knowledge that in twenty years it would itself be that of an old woman, was strong and beautiful as a figure carved in stone. It would be nice to ask her in, nice to look at that fine head for another half-hour. But it would not be appropriate. Or would it? Had she caught the flash of Betty's eyes looking at her in the driving mirror? It was hard to be sure at that distance.

Betty's glance into the mirror encountered a direct stare from Miss Stokoe and ricocheted back to the road. Thick with bloody traffic. With a sharp swing to the left, she shot into a near-empty lane, cutting off a cyclist, surging up to the lights. Betty was surprised that Miss Stokoe showed no nervousness of her driving. On the very few occasions she'd had another body in the car (Mother's to be precise) it'd been terrified. But perhaps to an old woman anything was better than the bus. How did Miss Stokoe's dolls legs mount bus steps designed, it would seem, for athletes? Betty cursed the fascists who ran London Transport. How would she get the basket in and out? Did she clamber in herself and then wait for someone to hand it to her?

There would be moments when she thought the bus was moving off, Jo-soap in her wicker prison still on the pavement. Did she then look around at the milling crowds of youth for someone to help her? Did she shrink from their barking voices, their pushing and shoving? If nobody gave her a seat, did she hang there, hating them? Betty cursed bus passengers for their seat-filling bottoms. And, as they heaved and sweated, did she think of the world this gilded youth was making — creating inflation to give themselves annual pay rises while it whittled away the savings of old schoolteachers; making a big deal of a ten-pound bonus at Christmas while they bankrupted the National Health Service? A ten-pound bonus: would Miss Stokoe put that towards a 5-minute plumber's visit costing thirty-five pounds; or did passing handymen keep, after a fashion, her house in one piece in between eyeing her teaspoons?

Beards, they would wear beards, those handymen. Betty had a particular horror of the grizzled hair curling away from damp pink lips, the little tongue darting behind — appalling images of female genitalia that dragged your eyes into their clamminess. All bodies were unpleasant, their soft parts revolting. And Betty was encumbered with one too, part of the baggage, along with Mother, furniture, bank accounts, things whirling in your head — things you had to drag with you through time, things every person passing in the street pressed deeper into your brain.

Betty held down her rage against the human race, curtailing it to a rattle of fingers on the driving wheel. Play, could it be play, that little escape through the fingers of anger? Miss Stokoe set store by play.

Had it been play, that terrible day, thirty years ago, which ended in all the other children refusing to play with her? Betty had wanted to play. Even Mother had said she could play with pretty blonde Maureen, because Maureen was the only other girl on the estate who didn't have lice in her hair. Nor could Maureen, newly rehoused, know that Mother and Betty were even poorer than the contemptibly poor people round them. Twelve-year old Betty, struck dumb with shyness, had followed Maureen for weeks. Maureen had a yellow ball. Betty had no toys because it would have been shameful for anyone to see her playing with rags.

One day Betty had picked up the ball — only to throw it, as the other children did. But she had done something wrong, squeezed it, kept it too long, something which ought not to have been done, for Maureen was on top of her trying to drag it away, and Betty — possessing for a few seconds the whole of Maureen's attention — was not letting it go. Then — how had it happened? — she was fighting to hold it, until there were tufts of blonde hair in her fingernails and her dress was spattered with blood. How could she have known that Maureen would be so soft and friable, crumple like a piece of silver paper in her hands? Maureen had cried and screamed. Betty hadn't cried; she never cried: not for the ruined dress, not for the beating, not for Maureen whom she would never follow any more. When Jo-soap began to play, had she also begun to cry?

Betty sneaked another glance at the mirror. Miss Stokoe was smiling. She was a fool. Worse, she was a lying fool, lying to herself, letting herself in for more torture. How could she smile when she was no use any more; when nobody but an aged cat kept alive on anabolic steroids wanted her; when the whole world looked on her as a burden? Most smiles were snakes, glittering with deceit. This smile was worse, a worm craving indulgence. The tyres squealed as Betty swung into Valley Road, a street of imposing Victorian houses. She looked out for the most delapidated.

As the car's movements became less certain, Miss Stokoe leaned forward. 'That's it; the house just beyond the corner.' It had been a thrilling drive. She would have liked it to go on forever. It would be wonderful to fly up one of those fast new roads that Ellen had called Motor-Ways, up to a place where Jo could smell the sea, with this woman who handled the powerful machine as if were an extension of her body.

Deftly as she could, she got out. 'So kind.' Betty had taken out the basket. 'Thank you, I would be grateful if you took her up the steps. Jo weighs almost nothing, but the basket is cumbersome.'

Betty held the basket high, clear of the cold step, while Miss Stokoe rummaged for her key. The door stuck as usual. Betty's free hand reached over her head and eased it open; then, to Miss Stokoe's pleasure, she followed her into the kitchen, standing still as a sentry while Miss Stokoe cleared a space on the table for the basket. Better still, Betty's strong brown hands lifted out the rabbity little form; they prized open the mouth.

'Dry. Could you get her something to drink.'

Miss Stokoe filled up her best china bowl and watched while Jo drank greedily and Betty, with the abstracted air of a soldier giving water to an injured comrade, tilted the bowl towards her. Miss Stokoe fiddled with the buttons of her tweed coat; it felt tight; she felt hot; she was swamped with longing. She wanted Betty to sit down.

She wanted to talk to her. Not about ordinary things, not about the cost of the special cat food she now had to buy or her fear of falling in the bathroom and not being able to call. She wanted to tell her the story of her life: it was a love story. She wanted to tell how love had infused her whole life from the time Ellen had come to her room at the Normal College half a century before. She wanted to tell what one could never quite tell except perhaps hidden in playful stories about small things. To tell how sometimes, even now, when dreams had been kind, while Jo-soap sprawled snoring on her stomach, she woke to hear the points of her breasts calling for Ellen's touch. To tell how this was not painful, not really painful, but thrilling, that her body which had long ceased to be full and joygiving was still singing its love song.

Betty took the china bowl to the sink and looked about for some clear space to put it down. Miss Stokoe's bespectacled glance followed. 'Jo looks so much brighter now, my dear,' she said. Pleasure ran through her veins, down to her very fingertips. 'Doesn't she have a glorious purr? How very competent you are.'

'It's the jab,' said Betty, who had turned her attention to the leaking tap. 'The effect won't last. You should feed her now.'

Betty bolted while the cat was sucking up a stodge of canned animal — another cat for all one knew — they were such shits the petfood manufacturers. The wet-rot swollen door she pulled roughly to. Her heart banged against her ribs. She took a gulp of air to clear the catpee-catsick stink out of her nostrils, replace it with petrol-fumes. Her eyes raked the skyline, scraping them clear of the images of greasy cobwebs against a tangle of TV aerials. For one awful moment she had thought that Miss Stokoe was going to do something — laugh, take her hand, cry — do something unbearable. Betty wanted to leap into the car and roar up the motorway, faster and faster, get the hell out of it. She wanted to race the cold wind, on and on, up to dunes whistling with marram grass.

But she didn't. She drove home. She did the washing up for Mother. When Mother asked about her day she said, as always, that nothing had happened. There was nothing to be said about the run-down surgery; nothing to say about almost being made a Joe Soap of by two geriatrics. She made no enquiries about Mother's day. Then she watched some rubbish on the telly for an hour before bed.

The Hockey Club

Janet must have been a clubbable type. In her first term at the University of Natal, Pietermaritzburg campus, in the marvellous year of 1960 when all the world was just waiting to be remade, she had joined the lot pretty well. The Catholic Students Association, The Rag Week Support Group, the Bach Cantata Club and the banned Communist Party. But, although at school she had been a ferocious right half renowned for her black-and-blue shins, she had not joined the Hockey Club.

This was a decision taken after thought. Janet, aged seventeen and aware of her farm-school education as a ball and chain around her ankles, had a mission: she wanted to become a Real Person. A career she thought little about — unless there was some way she could be a student forever. Her subject of study was already an embarrassment; she had turned the Administration Section upside down by asking to change from chemistry to English literature. What she wanted was what she saw in the clever women arguing in the junior common room about the poetry of St John of the Cross. She wanted to sidle up to them in the hope that something sayable would come into her head, something which would make someone stop short and say — 'Well, the infant has a point.'

On one such occasion, when she was dangling after an argument, as silent as someone who at school had been a chatterbox could unnaturally find herself, it had all become a little clearer. In the middle of a pregnant pause, the Hockey Club burst in. After a famous victory. Eleven huge women, smelling of sweat, linseed oil and African dust, arms linked, goalie Sandy McGillivray with her massive calves still encased in cricket pads, they stopped a dozen Gauloises in mid-puff.

'We won, we won,' they sang. 'We smashed the Japies into the middle of next week.' And then, as the murmur of conversation faded: 'All together now:

> We're a hungry pack of hound dogs,
> Baying for a fight;
> You're a sprawling heap of cat guts —
> Twinset, pearls and tights.
> So! — get your sticks up for the bully-off
> We'll run you through tonight.

Into the silence that ensued, someone uttered: 'Yuk!' And that was the cruel truth of it.

Winter drew on. The dust, briefly anchored by the morning mist, then liberated, cracked lips, powdered library books and spread the scent of hockey even into the basement lecture theatre. Janet was not doing very well. Becoming a Real Person seemed further away than ever. She was reading, with frenzy, everything the clever women read, but it came together in no world view. She dressed herself in smocks and lyle stockings and acquired a taste for cheap dry Stellenbosch wine, but even so she knew she was a fraud. Not an interesting fraud; just below par.

She had, after a fashion, a minor place: she now disbelieved in God but admired the ritual of the Mass; her unpowerful mezzo voice had come in handy to pad out the contraltos at the Bach Cantata Club; she learned to simper at the men as well as the best of them, and Joanna Swinderby (whose dissertation on Simone Weil had virtually assured her of a scholarship to some great university in the Mother Country) spoke kindly to her. Such were her achievements. Winter was dry and cold and she hoped without much hope that her melancholy was the sign of a sensitive soul.

They were hard at it, on the playing fields outside the library window. The crash of oiled wood in the bully-off, the thumping of the hard earth, the groans as Sandy McGillivray foiled yet another lunge towards the goal. Janet's pencil wound its weary way through *Piers Ploughman*. Then someone, with a left hook, a short pass and a thrust, broke through the impenetrable McGillivray. It was a goal. Papers all over the library fluttered in the roar as the women out there under the sky flung their arms around each other and McGillivray picked up the ball, spat on it, rubbed it against her groin and gently rolled it centre-field. Janet was thoughtful. Sandy McGillivray had not been well served by her right half. Janet would have foreseen that attack. Joanna Swinderby, partitioned off from Janet by a mountain of books, looked up and muttered, 'One has to preserve oneself, avoid wasting energy by rather hating sport.'

It was June, and the corn was green in Piers Ploughman's Malvern Hills. It was June, and the parched African grass was grazed down to its roots by hockey sticks.

That evening, in the privacy of her room, Janet hauled down her trunk. A pair of canvas boots, the rubber studs over the ankles much scuffed: she took them out. They still fitted. But the rough worsted skirt with her name inked in on the label fell to her knees. The Hockey Club women's skirts barely covered their knickers. She measured the skirt against herself and had to admit that she saw a ridiculous figure in the mirror. It was not difficult to imagine McGillivray's scorn if this object were to make its way down the slope to the playing fields, then stand on the sidelines, waiting to be asked to join in. The whole thing was misconceived.

As they massed outside the dining hall, waiting for the gong, Janet studied the notices: a jumble sale to raise funds towards the legal expenses of political prisoners; treble recorder players wanted by the Early Music Group; open hockey practice before breakfast the following morning. No, it was quite clear the whole thing was most definitely misconceived; she would not go. At table, she joined the group talking about Virginia Woolf.

'No, not art. Definitely not,' someone said, 'It's all self-consciousness and strain delivering only — 'she folded back the sleeves of her undergraduate gown to keep them out of her soup ' — yards and yards of self-consciousness and strain.'

'Indeed,' chimed in another, 'like peeling an onion: you strip off the layers and there's nothing in the middle.'

Janet ventured: 'But don't you like *The Years*, even?'

'That tedious imitation of Tolstoy. No.'

Janet thought of the passage where the ardent, clumsy Rose asks Maggie to join her at a suffragist meeting. When Maggie, so beautiful, so self-contained, so unreachable, looks up from her needlework to say with a smile, No she would hate it. When Rose takes in with the force of a blow that someone she likes very much will never like her. If there was nothing in the middle of that, it was the nothing of tragedy.

Janet persevered. 'You don't like Rose, just Rose?'

'I suppose there's the germ of an idea there,' came from the more conciliatory Joanna Swinderby, 'but the style is so laboured one loses interest in her.'

Janet had scarcely been able to put the book down. She had felt so terribly sorry for Rose that she wanted to tear right into the pages, to seize Rose by the hand and say, 'But *I* like you, Rose.' Janet's tastes were clearly immature. She added nothing further on that or any other subject.

Across the hall, the Hockey Club was celebrating somebody's birthday with a crate of beer. They were rowdier than ever, and there was even more than usual of the throwing of arms around each other. An occasional sniff of distaste came from Janet's table. 'But *I* like you, Sandy McGillivray,' Janet let herself think.

The Hockey Club was impossible. Yet, at six-thirty the following morning, Janet was scrambling down the slope to the playing fields, wearing a hockey skirt which had been roughly tacked up to the level of her knickers. With its unironed hem, it stood out like a little wheel. A low mist rolled along the ground, making the world vague, white and silent.

As she drew level she saw movement at the far field, as of a herd of wildebeest coupling. Coming closer, a voice:

'And-a nine, and-a ten, and RE-lax.'

The women doing press-ups collapsed with their faces in the dust. Sandy McGillivray, at the head, was still perched in the up position, her powerful arms and rigid cricket boots raising her whole body clear of the ground. She was afloat on a river of mist. Janet moved up to the foot of the herd.

After a slow passage of minutes, McGillivray got to her feet and began stomping towards her, kicking up fragments of dying grass. Janet slung her hockey-stick rifle-wise over her shoulder and stood her ground.

McGillivray approached and looked her over.

'Lost our blue stockings in the laundry, have we?' she said, studying Janet's goosepimpled knees.

There being no possible answer to this, Janet folded her arms over her stick and stared at the fringe of trees behind McGillivray's ginger head.

'I suppose you want to play?'

'Yes.'

'Well — you obviously haven't got the speed for a winger. There's no way you could have the personality for a forward; you couldn't raise the power for a back. And I'm the only goalie on this scene. So what's your position?'

'Half.'

'Uh-huh. Are you any good?'

'I played for the first team at school.'

'What school?'

Janet flushed. 'Umtentweni Rural Government Secondary.'

Sandy McGillivray grinned. 'Sounds a godforsaken place.'

Janet flushed again: 'Our school got into the quarter finals of the southern district section of the inter-school championship in 1955.'

'Well done. What did you play then, school mascot?'

'Junior linesman.' It had been her first year at Umtentweni; it had been a glorious year. The big girls who played in that wonderful game had hung their green and orange colours all over the truck that brought them to the City of Pietermaritzburg where there were traffic lights. And afterwards they had sung school songs and spirituals all the miles of dirt road home, Janet and the other juniors rocking in the arms of the players, feeling the River Jordan and the River Umzimkulu merge one great flow. Janet looked up at McGillivray. She was, for once, not ashamed of her school.

'So, in 1955, when you were still in nappies, your school almost won a quarter of a cup. You could say, for the sake of argument, I'm impressed. Since it happens I could use a right half.'

Janet nodded, thinking of the lamentable performance she had seen through the library window.

'Okay then, half. We don't hang about here like your literary ladies. Fall in. We've got to build a lot of muscle before breakfast, and my God you could use a bicep or two.'

Janet, her face in the dust; Janet, guilty of the saggiest of press-ups, her nicotine-coated lungs bursting after the first 100-yard sprint; and-a nine, and-a ten and RE-lax. Janet felt her heart soar like a bird. At breakfast, she went in and sat with the dusty, sweaty gang.

But that was the easy one. The literary ladies never got up for breakfast.

A World Apart

'My God, Connie, you look terrible!'

Connie's glance took in the row of wine goblets hanged by their feet, crazed reflections from the cut glass mirror of the barman scratching his ass, and then, travelling over coiffures rumpled by a day's dogfights in the boardroom, the shocked face of her friend.

'Good.' She pushed a tumbler of vodka across the table towards her; her own was already empty. 'I feel terrible.'

Then, before the other woman was seated '— Because Helga's got another lover. Has had for some little time.' She paused, then added savagely: 'For the past seventeen years to be precise.'

'What!' The word ripped through the thick air of the pub.

'Just that. Meet Connie Casparius, mistress, for six whole months, of a middle-aged yuppie. Park your coat, for heaven's sake, or are you dashing off again?'

'Connie, I...'

Connie stared at the flushed, pained face. '"I" what? That "I" swallowed a pack of lies. So did the whole bloody community.'

'I ... don't know what to say. It's not possible.'

'It bloody is. And you're an even bigger fool than me if you can't see now how the whole thing was staring us in the face from the word go.'

'Connie, I'm so sorry. I mean I can't believe it — you're so close, and so incredibly good for each other. This is just awful.'

'Yup.' Connie threw a hostile look at eyes that were brimming with sympathy. 'Now quit rabbiting and get me another drink.'

Alone for a few minutes, Connie immediately forgot her friend, and sank like a stone into her pain. She felt nothing against Helga's lover, no anger, not even any jealousy. She didn't, at that moment, even feel anything against Helga. Around and around her head flooded the same words that, for the past twenty four-hours, had swirled over her brain while her breath pounded in frenzy to push away these enclosing waters: 'Why did you lie to me, Helga? Why didn't you believe in my love? Why didn't you trust me enough to tell me?'

And if Helga had? Could they then have worked something out? Could they, all of them, have been friends? Would they have gone together to the opera? — Pointless, childish questions, which could not have been answered anyway, because the real Helga was never there. 'I'm in love' Connie muttered out loud, looking straight into the face of a man glancing slyly at her over his gin and tonic, 'With a woman who doesn't exist.'

By the time a fresh drink was in her hand, Connie was ready to tell the story — not the story of their love affair, that had already been told, many times, in pubs much prettier than this one, to friends who were bowled over with joy, or with envy, at Connie's happiness.

This story started innocently enough, yesterday, at the headquarters of the Industrial Finance Corporation plc, where Connie slaved and Helga managed. They were in the lift, on the drop down from the canteen, and it stopped at the sixth floor. Helga folded down her long body to give Connie a peck on the cheek then got off, leaving Connie with Miss Richards, the archivist.

'What a nice young friend you are for Helga,' Miss Richards said, while Connie grinned amiably. 'And of course she does so need friends at this time.' Connie gave a slight frown. It was a good time, a brilliant time.

'Mind you, for my money, friends should tell her that she brought it on herself,' Miss Richards rambled on: 'It was she who persuaded the girl she could sing. Until talents are put to the test, parents are blind, I rather think, to the limitations of their daughters.'

The lift door opened, then shut again. 'Pardon?'

'Yes — witch, sailor, queen, what you will, it takes more than a gift for mimicry to make comedy in an opera. And now, with a fortnight till the church packs with people who have forgotten the feel of a pew, Mother has stage fright.'

Miss Richards had been with the Corporation far too long, twice as long as Helga, who had anyway moved steadily up the career ladder, while Miss Richards mouldered in the basement archives. 'You must be thinking of someone else,' said Connie with a smile. 'Helga doesn't keep a witch, sailor, queen or daughter' (adding to herself, 'except when I'm all of them.')

Miss Richard's smiled back. 'I stand corrected. An old dog doesn't easily learn new tricks of phrase like "co-parent".'

Did the lift suddenly fall two floors? Miss Richards was still chatting as if everything was normal. Long past her own exit, Connie followed Miss Richards out at the basement. 'What did you say this girl's name was?'

'Tosca. I would have preferred Mimi, and Carmen would have suited the little gypsy, but they chose to name her after a raving murderess. Of course, one has to make allowances. Nothing is quite as one would expect when two women bring up a child.'

Miss Richards, who had a perfectly good computer in the library, began to riffle through the index cards she still preferred to use. 'I won't say "children should be seen and not heard", but Helga does indulge the girl in some rather inappropriate performances.' She looked up sharply, 'You know, don't you that Tosca's singing the witch in *Dido and Aeneas*?' (Connie rolled her head vaguely.)

'Yes, witch. Mind you, it has its side: did you hear about the time the MD descended to one of his official visits, and found Tosca, perched on the top shelves, yelling "Destruction's our delight"? My dear, you can't imagine...'

Connie couldn't imagine. She said drably: 'She sounds a right pest.'

'No.' Miss Richards's smile was benign. 'She has nice manners, and that's rare enough these days. She just spends too much time in the company of adults.' Miss Richards plucked out the card for *Voice Projection Made Simple*. 'Helga used to bring her in here to do her homework. I did my best to make good their neglect of her grammar and spelling. But I'm detaining you with my chatter, my dear. You need a book on... ?'

'She doesn't come here any more, that girl — at least not for the past six months?'

'A year, in effect, due to a rather unfortunate incident.' Miss Richards laid a grave hand over the index cards as if to close up their ears. 'One of Tosca's classmates was assaulted — brutally, intimately I mean to say — on her way home from music practice. Helga didn't tell you? I suppose these things are rather painful. Anyway, the culprit was never found — that was why they decided to move to the country, that village near Saffron Walden. I rarely see Tosca now. Such a pity. The girls at her new school sing like Miss Piggy, she says. She'd love to spend the week in town, going to Covent Garden of an evening. Helga's little *pied à terre* is easily big enough for two, don't you think?'

Connie did. She knew the capacity of the little *pied à terre* well. It was what she thought of as home.

Straining against the press in the pub, Connie's friend wore a stricken expression, as if her scarf was binding her throat. Suddenly irritated, Connie snapped: 'Sing something other than "I'm sorry", will you, just to change the tune.'

She watched her friend swallow. 'I was thinking, Connie: if you put up a fight, you've got to get her. Seventeen years — God — the core of that relationship must have dried out ages ago. Helga's mad about you; and she knows, like everybody else, that she's grown ten years younger through being with you. I guess its breaking up anyway, Helga's thing with — with — '

'I don't know the woman's bloody name. Her letters to Helga are signed "DouDou", followed by a big X. She writes just about every day. Screeds of stuff about a family of badgers on the bank, about "tempting the slugs" by planting lettuces, and, of course, endless twitch about Tosca's singing in that bloody opera. Forget the odd throwaway about being lonely in a big bed.'

'Helga showed you the letters?'

This was the first intelligent thing Connie had heard that evening. She acknowledged this with a nod. 'No. I collected *Voice Projection* from Miss Richards, and left the office. Didn't even say I was taken sick or something. I went to the bloody *pied à terre* and picked through everything of Helga's. Unlike Helga, "DouDou" has a perfectly legible, if pretentiously copperplate, hand — '

'Oh, I get it now: that explains Helga going off to the family every weekend.' (Connie noted that the penny was dropping.) 'It was that kind of family. I never thought...'

Connie ignored the interruption. '— Except for her capital 'S's, which she shapes like treble clefs. Then I put the letters in a Sainsbury's bag, packed my things and dragged them back to my place. Helga came round after work. I handed her the book and all the presents she'd given me, plus DouDou's letters which were no longer of any interest.'

Connie's friend was churning. 'It must have been something to see someone smooth as Helga caught with her fingers in the till,' she said desperately. 'I hope you made her crawl.'

'She started to mutter some stuff about waiting for the right moment to tell me because, apparently, I'm hasty in my judgments. I thanked her for the insult, which was at least honest, and told her she'd treated me like dirt and DouDou like bloody shit. I didn't let her in to crawl.'

'Or to try to sort something out? I mean, this can't be the end; you've got to negotiate. And, after all, Connie, Helga's facing a heavy number: a child is a serious commitment.'

'*I* am a serious commitment.' Connie pushed her glass, again empty, across the table, and watched the good old friend, who was now nothing to her, almost leap to the bar to have it refilled, anxious, no doubt, to escape.

'Oh, hell,' Connie said to herself, 'why am I torturing the poor woman like this. She's threshing around trying to find some way to help. And Christ I need friends. I just don't give a toss about her, I don't give a toss about anything, not about Helga, not even about me. What has loving Helga done to my brain that the whole world is a load of shit because she's a load of shit?'

But then, Connie reminded herself, she had known all along that Helga was full of shit. She'd even quite liked the feeling that she was knocking it out of Helga. The woman used to vote Conservative, for a start, and she hadn't got to be marketing manager for nothing. That was perfectly clear when Connie (her guts wrenched almost to nausea), had to watch while the MD kneaded the shoulder pads of Helga's jacket with his ham-red hand, and Helga beamed back her cheque book smile. Even now, the thought of that hand made hers bunch into a fist. Helga had no right to be so beautiful, and something so beautiful had no right to be so corrupt.

So why did she love her? How did it happen that, when Helga smiled her other smile, and said: 'I see it differently now, darling, you've opened a whole new world for me,' Connie believed, and found, herself, a whole new world in Helga's long arms? Even now, even now, when there was nothing left to believe in, if Helga walked in through the door, she could still fall into those arms, and then she would find relief in tears.

At closing time Connie, who had sat alone with her vodka from about 9.30 (having released her friend to go feed her cats), stumbled into the street to fight for a taxi. Out of the English National Opera flooded wave after wave of faces flushed with emotion borrowed from fictions of love and pain. Stony faced, Connie shoved two men aside to hijack a cab.

A little earlier that night, Helga, her long legs squeezed under the table in the bay of the *pied à terre*, her uneaten supper dumped beside DouDou's letters in a plastic bag, was making her third or fourth attempt to write a letter of her own, to Connie. A drink might have helped, but later that night she would drive up to Saffron Walden. There was nothing, and everything, to say.

She smoothed out one crumpled ball and read:

> Darling, I can't begin to tell how bitterly I regret having — though unintentionally — misled you. You wrong me to say this came out of lack respect. I always meant to tell you. I was giving the timing of it a great deal of thought because I appreciated the seriousness of your...

This was meant to sound persuasive, cool with an undertone of caring; it came out as the blabber of a criminal in the dock. She pushed her spectacles up into her hair, and leaned back.

Connie's face through the half-open door, flaming with fury, came into her mind. Helga had so often seen Connie angry, and had always, until then, found it touching. Connie's rosebud mouth (one of her charms was that she never knew how pretty she was) would constrict itself to a hard line of muscle, her neat little teeth biting the ends off her words. And Helga would laugh at the ire hurled at politicians or police, or just generally at men, and say 'And tomorrow we die.' Did this show this lack of respect? Perhaps it did. Helga had thought of it as tenderness. It certainly showed lack of imagination that she never realized how painful it would be to find that anger turned on her. Yet, even now, while she winced at the recollection of Connie's glare, her whole body throbbed with desire for her. Was this also lack of respect?

Yet hadn't her whole connection with Connie come out of respect, at least out of Connie giving her a new respect for herself? It was difficult, now, to take herself back into the vacancy that was her life before Connie.

Libby — her 'DouDou' (Connie had made the word sound like an obscenity) — had so contentedly created her new country life, in which Helga was a visitor. Helga had found no new life at the *pied à terre*. She saw their old friends, all couples, sometimes; felt awkward, skinless somehow; drank too much. After a few months they rang less often to ask if Helga was all right, and Helga didn't ring at all. Instead, she asked Miss Richards to supper, and Miss Richards chatted about Tosca while Helga fretted, telling herself to accept with grace that Libby, not she, was the lifemaker. She put in a request for a transfer to the Corporation's new branch at Cambridge (but had no energy to push it through) and thought of her retirement, only fifteen years ahead. At Saffron Walden at the weekends, she helped the gardener clean out the ditches. In the evenings, she fine-tuned the recorder to give Libby and Tosca perfect playbacks of their rehearsals, and her car, to get it up to ever higher speeds on the M11. She scarcely tried to tune her brain which felt, not unhappy, but missing both the bass and high treble vibrations. It seemed a stable state, able to go on forever.

But in bounced Connie, the not particularly skillful computer operator who demanded to be consulted over every detail of the distribution lists then, without consultation, retitled all the women on it 'Ms'. Connie's arrival brought more banter, less work to the computer room, but Helga felt no need to stop it. She was amused, even when this girl made shameless advances in view of the entire Corporation at the lofty, middle-aged marketing manager.

Helga warmed day by day, in a weak moment even accepting one of Connie's invitations to lunch. To her surprise, Connie had booked a table at a smart little French restaurant, where she ordered snails and then needed Helga's help to deal with them. They argued (and Helga laughed) about feminism until it got to be so late there wasn't much point in rushing back. Helga couldn't resist, after the brandy, reaching out a hand to touch the downy cheek, and finding herself, to her shame, excited to see Connie blush.

'You only like me', said Connie severely, 'because I make you feel like a big number.' Connie couldn't know that until that day, Helga felt like no number at all but a big round O.

Helga turned back to the crumpled page, to the paragraph where the handwriting become agitated.

> ...I didn't lie to you as such. You didn't ask. I didn't tell. It was you who always insisted that we have our separate spaces, and you who wanted to keep her separate life. You gave no account to me of what you did with the friends you met every weekend and several times during the week. This was your stipulation, and I am surely permitted an equivalent freedom, even if I interpret it differently. Bear in mind that fifteen years divide us, and a wholly different set of mores. Since we talk about respect, was I, in your scenario, to become the doll in the cupboard while you played with other toys? Was I, but not you, to be denied a world apart?

Again, Helga pushed up the spectacles. This could rate as reasoned argument, but was untrue. Connie *had* let Helga into her life, into the messy, muddled, fascinating, po-faced, vividly alive world which had been, for Helga, at first a farce and then a renaissance. Connie had taken Helga into her 'community' of ardent young women who ate beans and wore dreadful clothes, but whose arguments rang like iron, even if sometimes like the cacophonous orchestra of the steelworks. Connie had volunteered 'to totally deconstruct then totally reconstruct' her, yet giggled like a girl when Helga said that sounded rather naughty. Connie had dragged her to any number of bars, where women gathered in throngs of ten or more, kissing and dancing and answering back at the cabaret; to fringe theatres where the curtains were scented with cannabis, even to long debates at Wesley House, where 'lesbian' acquired an 'ism', making what had been to Helga an unsayable word into a whole brave new way of thinking.

And it was Connie who had insisted that they make no vows, not because there were to be no rules, but because the statement of them would take the power from the spirit to the letter. This was the trust Helga had abused. 'I'm sorry Connie,' she muttered to herself, 'I did want it to be the way you believed and I half believed it was.'

Helga turned back to the letter: 'Dear girl, think what you are doing; you are throwing to the winds the great pleasure we make for each other. Everything between us has been so sweet; how can something so innocent do harm?'

Once again, Connie's mouth, angelic under the tangled curls, came to her: Connie displaying the banner she had painted for a lesbian pride march; Connie laughing loud at Helga's fears that a newspaper photographer might splash that banner, Connie and Helga beneath it, for all the Corporation to see; Connie challenging her with being ashamed of her life.

And so Helga marched under the banner, side by side with Connie, through the streets of Holborn. At first shrinking, after heady dousings with sunshine, the noisy camaraderie of her young companions, the cheerful invitations yelled at policewomen in the line to join them, and several cans of lager on the hoof, Helga felt like a child at the start of the summer holidays.

And that night, the lovely girl slithered down Helga's body blasted with the gales of freedom, licking off the sweat and the fear until Helga quite forgot that this was an inexpert, clumsy lover, and every nerve knew only what came from that mouth. It was after that that the momentous words had fallen from her lips: 'I love you, Connie.'

Helga screwed the paper into a tight ball and threw it towards the sink in the little kitchenette. It missed. She got up to retrieve it, but instead poured herself a scotch, a small one. She could drive up in the morning, but then she would have to phone, and now, for the first time since she'd started the affair with Connie, it was impossible to speak to Libby.

She could do the one thing that could save them: Jump into the car right now, drive like the clappers, plan no set speech but let the whole story pour into ears that had listened patiently to so many of her troubles. Tonight, she could tell Libby that she was in love with Connie. Then tomorrow, she could perhaps have Connie in her arms again.

But was she in love? What would it amount to, this love, when the claws in the guts were sheathed? What then would she make of a bunch of women who were too proud to work for men, but queued at the Social Security offices for the scrapings of male taxes? What would be left of love if she lost Libby, or kept her, but wounded for life? Could she sacrifice Tosca, who, hurling her stentorian soprano at the world as if its ears were thick with wax, made Helga tremble with the need to shield her? Could she bring real death to a little opera sung in a village church?

And if she did tell, what would she ask: that Libby should be patient, wait till the fever had died? What then could be left, between her and Libby, of the 'respect' Connie set such store by? If Libby knew, as Connie now knew, of her infidelity, how could Libby respect Helga? Was it merely to win back Connie's respect that it seemed necessary to tell Libby? Or was it, in fact, merely to increase Connie's power, to complete a triangle, that she had to tell Libby?

Helga paced up and down, the whisky rocking in the glass. All this talk of 'respect' now seemed fraudulent, no more than a bravado display of its frailty by an ego so overblown as to be surprised to find in itself any imperfection. Helga downed her drink at a gulp. This 'respect', she announced to herself, amounted to nothing more than intrusion into people's private places.

Because it sometimes seemed to Helga that Libby already knew. Occasionally, in her letters, there were lines that made Helga cold with fear. But nothing followed from these hints and it occurred to Helga that if Libby knew, she chose to leave that knowledge in the private places.

Mostly, though, Libby's uncertainty was full of innocence. She wrote soulfully about the temptations Helga faced, alone in the city during the week. 'I see somebody going for you,' she would write, 'because you're even more beautiful now than you were seventeen years ago.' And Helga, all her fluids infused with Connie's, recognized that she had become beautiful to Libby, with a beauty that would crumble to dust if Libby knew what power had changed her.

Helga, young, had an uncompleted look, vacant somehow. In middle age, the hardening of her bones made the hollows Connie had taken for depth. And Connie's hands had smoothed those hollows, giving to Helga what felt like real depth. At those times, arriving at Saffron Walden, she knew that she too had her secret spring and felt, for the first time in seventeen years, Libby's equal.

Libby had always had her secret places. Now she had made them into a world. She wrote with delight about her music room overlooking the badger bank, where her pupils vied with the arpeggios of blackbirds while her daughter tried out a new instrument every week. Helga was told about this world, but not invited into it. Libby, without Helga, was in perfect harmony with a society of commuter's wives grieving across fences for husbands chained to desks in the city. All this (for Libby's thoughts would pour, in an unbroken stream onto the page) Libby would relate during long evenings in the ramshackle attic still smelling of apples that she had converted into a study for the sole purpose of writing to her lover. Libby loved her world apart.

And so Helga knew that Libby loved her more for having leisure to miss her. Helga believed she was the centre of Libby's dreams. But fantasies feed on want, not fulfilment. Perhaps all those commuters' wives leaning on the fences believed their husbands had lovers in the city; perhaps they even wanted to think this, to lower themselves into a private pain where washing lines dwindled to half-remembered dreams and they were sister to the earthworm speared on a garden fork. When Libby missed her 'with a sharpness, sometimes, that takes my breath away', Helga could tell herself that her affair with Connie (which was after all not designed to be serious) was lifegiving to them all.

But Tosca made her feel uncomfortable: Tosca was as near in age to Connie as Connie was to Helga. And she was disconcertingly like Connie: so definite, so unconscious of herself, of the grand naivety of the great statements through which she would change the world. Was it because of something Helga exuded of Connie that Tosca had recently become interested in sex, in a rather appallingly dispassionate way? Tosca would repeat the maidens' foolish gush about the handsome Prince Aeneas, then say, 'Dido shouldn'ta gone for all that stuff. It's so damn gluey.'

Helga could, with difficulty, conceive of telling Libby about Connie, but with Tosca, what lay between her and Connie seemed shabby and shameful.

But not with Libby? Why was she now inventing for herself a secret conspiracy with Libby in the having of secrets? Why couldn't she just admit that Libby's private world, like Connie's, was a child's garden, hers a wilderness of deceit? Helga interrupted her pacing, up and down the small space of the *pied à terre*, to pour herself another, slightly larger, scotch.

It had never occurred to Helga that she might break up with Libby, but she had, more than once, thought of ending it with Connie. There was the Friday evening a few weeks back when she arrived at the cottage to find Libby almost inside the belly of the piano, trying to track down a broken string. 'Oh, baby,' Libby said, 'Beethoven broke strings trying to make his deaf ears hear music; I can't make my blind eyes see this wire.' Helga fetched a flashlight, pliers and her spectacles. Libby hadn't thought to do any of these things.

Why had Libby been pounding the piano so violently? Unlike her daughter's, Libby's touch was silken. Helga probed, fearful of unearthing a pain that was to do with Connie. But Libby, mistress of diplomacy, would say only that she needed Helga around more often to take care of her.

So, after they fitted the new string, but before tuning it, Libby drew her lover down onto the Chinese carpet, and in those minutes it came to Helga that there was between her and Libby something so deep that neither of them knew where the bottom of it was.

Helga had kept Libby in ignorance for something more than a secret, more than shame. A voice in her that was not argument said that what she had done was betrayal of Libby's faith in their love, and that faith had, for seventeen years, given Helga's life its substance. Helga flung open a window to let out some of the heat now burning her cheeks. How dare Connie claim a right to know when Libby was still in ignorance? How dare Connie talk about respect when what she wanted was to become a partner in a crime against Libby?

It was over. Connie had ended it. Circumstances had given Connie the dignity of putting in the knife. That was respect: to leave Connie the moral high ground. Well, she could keep it; she had no right to ask more.

Helga flung the remains of the scotch down the sink, and seized a fresh sheet of paper.

'Connie,' she wrote furiously:

> I accept your decision. It is over. We now both regard the matter as closed. I trust that you will say nothing at the Corporation and make no attempt to communicate with my family. Helga.

Without rereading, Helga thrust the sheet into an envelope, slammed on a stamp, grabbed her keys, and left the *pied à terre*, stopping briefly at the first posting box on the way to Saffron Walden, not turning back, even when she remembered that she had left the window wide. A burglar would be welcome to whatever dross she had left behind in London.

'Did you hear that young Tosca's performance as the witch evoked paeans of praise from the *Saffron Walden Gazette*?' Miss Richards said cheerfully as the lift lowered them gently down from the canteen.

'Uh — no, wonderful.' Connie looked at her watch which told her, as if she needed to know, that it was three months and two days since Helga had left the London office.

'Yes, they said it was gloriously "over the top". Would you like to come down to the archives to see the clipping the dear girl sent me? Autographed, it was, by herself in a fancy new signature made up of musical notations, with the capital T an embellished treble clef.'

'How original. That was in — ah — *Dido*?'

'Yes, poor Dido. The same journalist thought Libby was too old for such a demanding part. Must have been rather hurtful. Libby had a fine voice a few years ago.'

Connie felt blood rise to her cheeks. 'I'm sure it's still very fine.'

'More than adequate for a singing teacher, my dear, and we the old must learn to make room for you the young. Now dear Tosca — '

Connie's attempt to respond to Miss Richards's smile increased the now habitual pain in her chest which made her feel twice as old as Miss Richards. 'Journalists don't understand music,' — she broke in with surprising warmth — 'if Libby wasn't up to the part, she would have known it long before any crap artist on a local rag. She would have made that bumptious little brat sing it.'

Miss Richards stepped back, her handbag, filled with what sounded like rocks, knocking against the wall of the lift. 'I didn't mean to sound rude. In fact, Tosca said Libby sang quite well.'

Connie scowled, but Miss Richards recovered quickly. 'Tosca's not bumptious, by the way,' she said softly. 'She sent a charming note, though I wish it had shown some improvement in her grammar and spelling.' The lift slowed, as if by habit, at what used to be Helga's floor. 'Tosca aims to get into Cambridge next year,' Miss Richards added as the lift continued its graceful slide, 'and to commute there with Helga.'

It was time to press the emergency button, anything to get away.

'Wouldn't that be nice for them both? And isn't it amazing that Helga got, not only the promotion she's always deserved, but the chance to run the new branch at Cambridge? Libby must be rather jealous with Tosca running around Helga these days. Of course, Helga is really the better model, being a woman of the world and all that.'

A man got on at the fifth floor and turned his eyes to the ceiling. 'But, alas, it can't be long,' Miss Richards continued in a whisper, 'before Tosca quite forgets the funny old archivist who once let her sing from the high shelves.'

At the fourth floor, Connie escaped. When she felt stronger, in a week, in a month, she would take Miss Richards to the opera, any opera except *Dido and Aeneas*.

She went back to her desk, where her fellow slaves of the distribution lists were in a great state about the new marketing manager. The issue: was this double of John Travolta married?

'Married or no, I'll go for him,' said one. 'What d'ya think, Connie?'

'Leave him alone', muttered Connie. 'Marriages are built of bricks. You'll only get hurt trying to break in.'

Everybody tittered. They all thought it was rather a shame how Connie Casparius, who could look quite dishy when she bothered to comb her hair, was turning into a sour old maid.

The Magdalen at Forty

She had two fortieth birthdays, as she had two of everything.

In one, there was a candlelit dinner at the Café Minuit followed by an unsteady walk home through the alleys of Hampstead, arms entwined with Bernie's, singing a Holst setting of Robert Bridges:

> O love I complain,
> Complain of thee often,
> Because thou dost soften
> My being to pain.

The unworthy tears the song brought to her eyes owed more to wine than to art, but Bernie, big hearted as she had always been through their more than a decade together, leaned down and kissed them away with sweetness.

The other birthday happened at the same time and in the same place. She chose more or less the same scallops, but the woman opposite her ordered nothing because ghosts can drink chablis and smoke little cigars, but they do not eat pepper steak. That meal was not really a meal at all, though waiters brought things and took them away. It was a conversation, the same conversation as always, through thousands and thousands of times. 'Why didn't you love me, Cynthia?'

'Because,' replied the ghost, in a low, musical voice, the 'r's' showing a touch of Scotland, 'you can't wrap your arms around a bloody soup.'

Now, aged forty and one day, with a hangover, with her life half over and in the knowledge that she had to stop thinking of herself as young, it was assessment time. She had to make herself think it through, will herself to gather up her strength, to live, to live in her life, not in another fifteen years of waiting.

She was in her garden, the beautiful garden she had made for Cynthia, north-facing, with its dark side near the house, its secret mossy places fringed with saxifrage over stone, rising, through bank on bank of berberis and ceanothus to a blaze of wild roses. With this garden she had made a pact: when a pair of hedgehogs moved in, on that day Cynthia would look over the wall saying, 'Hello Fartface, that change of address card you sent me ages ago turned up this morning. Having nothing better to do, I thought I'd look you up.'

Was that pact the reason that though the garden housed beetles and frogs and voles — so many forms of wildlife — there were no hedgehogs? If she seized all her courage and cancelled that contract, could she still love the garden? She took in the rowan tree, planted near the fence so that Cynthia's face would appear between its feathery branches, the escalonia a slight distance away so that prickles would not touch but Cynthia would be close enough to see the delicacy of its tiny pink trumpets. She thought of the toad under the square stone by the pond, panting, waiting; waiting for Cynthia to say to it: 'What's keeping ya Quasimodo, jump.'

No, without Cynthia she would probably not be able to bear the garden. Or could she now, at forty and a day, gather up her strength and will it so?

> An' wer't not for thee
> My glorious passion,
> My heart I could fashion
> To sternness, as he.

Was Bridges right? If she tore this sickness out of herself could she fashion a garden for God, or for Bernie?

These days she only became aware of it when it stopped, the garden's constant ground bass: the sound of chisel chipping at stone, of Bernie working away (no doubt not wearing the dust mask the doctor had prescribed); Bernie making, so much of the time, images of her lover. In Highgate Cemetery's new wing, she was a stone angel. At a computer factory in Livingston she was Peter Pan.

Most often, though (for Bernie was still a Catholic and got much of her work from the Church) she was the Virgin. Sometimes she held in her arms a baby, or a dead man, for Bernie also had skill at bidding up. Bernie would peer deep into faces marked with the Vow of Poverty, working up a commission for a modest seated Virgin into handsome monuments to the Madonna with Child, or better still, an inspiring Annunciation, or a powerful Pieta.

Right now, Bernie was working on a Magdalen. The chipping died away. Bernie would be coming to the window of her studio, would throw up the sash and call to her. She rested her trowel and waited.

'Still murdering slugs, petal?' Bernie's dark curly head, leaning far out of the window, was covered in white dust, a bear emerging from a beehive.

'And you? Still murdering marble?'

'Not too sure about that. Some blocks of stone don't die without a fight.' Bernie eased her shoulder muscles. 'I'm afraid, blossom, I'm going to have to ask you to model again in a few minutes; I've got a problem with the Magdalen's left ear that a dozen drawings hasn't solved.'

'I'll just go wash my hands.' She was relieved. Bernie hadn't asked her what she was thinking. For once she hadn't needed to lie to this good woman that she cheated on every day of her life.

She had been twenty-five when Cynthia broke into her life, bursting its seams, at that bar, the dingy place workmates had taken her to, to have a look at the queers. She saw men with coifs a little longer than the coifs of the men she was with, with pants a little narrower and gestures a little wider. There was lots of talking, laughing, teasing, flirting. The music was loud and raw, with heaving drums and the insistent whine of an electric guitar, to her an unfamiliar and unpleasant sound. The place was disturbing, repellant, and her frame vibrated with excitement. She found herself examining the very few women there. Two were leaning up against the bar nearby. They wore fishermen's sweaters and tight black trousers; each had a foot on the rail, elbows on the counter. They were utterly unconcerned by the giggles and whistles that came from the outer ring of spectators where she sat with her workmates; theirs seemed a world of unimaginable danger and freedom.

Then one of the women lifted her head in response to some shout from across the room and waved. Another remark, and then, into a pause, she said in a voice of an extraordinarily beautiful timbre: 'If that's all your head can give you, Johnnie my darling, you'd best go boil it for a cabbage.'

Those words had struck her like a blow on the skull, and from that moment, she could see or hear nothing but Cynthia. She had trailed after her like a dog. And redoubled her efforts when she found Cynthia to be lonely and struggling to kick a valium habit. And eventually she had won her — for five weeks.

Every second of those five weeks had been relived a thousand times. The end had been so clearly contained in the beginning, in the first time Cynthia had said: 'Could you make some small effort not to be quite so intense? Could you crack a joke or something?'

Or, as always in that beautiful low voice, 'I come back from the theatre late and tired, starving, and all you've got for me is more of that Holst whingeing on the record player. Did your mother never teach you to fry an egg? And if you have to drown out the entire block, couldn't it be something with a bit of guts for a change; what's wrong with Carl Orff?'

Or, 'It may surprise you to know this, but it's possible to get bored with dissolving in a great soft vulva. Why don't you do something to me for a change? What are you so damn scared of?'

Once it began in earnest, she had almost welcomed it, the destruction, emphasising the differences between them. Take Cynthia's mockery of the music she held so dear: '"O love, I complain", complain, complain. What's he complaining about? He'd complain much louder if love pushed off, wouldn't he? If it stopped letting him joyride on his precious feelings? Can't you see you're just a couple of wankers?'

There was no point in the 'if onlys'; if she had been less

useless, less frozen; if Cynthia had been less impatient, less unhappy; if they had learned to do ordinary things together; if that American journalist (wearing a fisherman's sweater and tight black pants) hadn't leaned over the bar to say to Cynthia, 'I liked your stage management of *Who's Afraid of Virginia Woolf?* When can I interview you about it?'

Or in the ending, to which she had gone like someone to a hospice: 'I need space, sausage; I need space from you. You give me breathing trouble. Go visit your mother for a week.' She had packed a little bag and taken Cynthia's money for a first class train ticket (then been at a loss to explain this extravagance to her parents). She hadn't cried. She had spent the week lying on the beach in the sun and the rain, or swimming out beyond the point to where the tide sucked like an octopus, in this wonderful sea that she would now never have the chance to show Cynthia.

She hadn't cried for Cynthia, but she had cried for herself after her father had taken her to see a new film called *Morgan*: when he had put an arm on her shoulder and said: 'Why is my eldest daughter turning into an old maid?'

The old maid had taken the train back (second class) knowing what she would find: tangled sheets, the American journalist's fisherman's sweater on the bedroom floor. In a little flutter of something — hardly jealousy; she was too numb for jealousy — she had thrown the sweater and the bedding out into the street below. That was the only thing in the last act that now gave her satisfaction.

That, and perhaps to some extent the closing scene for which she prepared all evening. Cynthia would be back from the theatre at about 10.30. Perhaps the American journalist would be with her. She could lay a table for three, bake a soufflé, get some wine. She could wear yellow shorts to show off her tan and talk brightly about the new sport of windsurfing. She could say 'we' in front of the journalist, and, in the early hours, insist on walking her back to her car. Or she could make a great row, poke out the other woman's eyes. But of course she would do none of these things. She gathered up her clothes from Cynthia's wardrobe and bathroom and packed them; she shaved her legs and plucked her eyebrows; she washed her hair and dressed with care in old maid's dove grey. She played the Holst. She thought of what Cynthia would say, what she would not be able to say.

Her stuff fitted into two suitcases, which she left downstairs with the concierge. Cynthia's gifts to her — they had been frequent and generous in their first days together — were left in a neat pile on the mattress: an onyx ring, put back into its box, a pale suede jacket, a Dutch fisherman's cap, *Flight from the Enchanter* by Iris Murdoch. She hesitated, then took back the novel, tucking between its pages a stolen photograph of Cynthia ordering an electrician off the set.

At 10.30 sharp, Cynthia came in, alone, dragging her feet like Quasimodo. They didn't kiss. They stood facing each other in the passage, half a yard apart. There was no blood in either of their faces.

'You'll never know how much of a shit I feel about doing this — ', Cynthia began.

'You'll never know how much of a shit you are.'

And that was that. It had been done. It was over. Cynthia had already booked her a room at the Northview Hotel and a taxi was waiting. No meal had been prepared, but then there wouldn't have been time to eat one. 'O love, I complain.'

That was about all there was of information. How had that slender fare nourished her imagination for fifteen years? How had it had become so habitual, so necessary; how could she ever hope to be free of it?

> Thou makest me fear
> The mind that createth,
> That loves not nor hateth
> In justice austere.

She had followed Cynthia at a distance, to Greece, to Italy, and then to London. She became a theatre librarian and kept watch on fringe productions, new plays in the provinces, B-movies, anything Cynthia might have had a hand in. Sometimes, in the street, at some chance resemblance — the shape of the back of a head, a walk, or, most powerful of all, a voice — she would have to grasp at any support to keep her balance. She acknowledged her mental state to be unhealthy. She put it to herself that she ought to go back to the bar to try to drive out this image with a new one, but her strength failed at the prospect of labouring to breathe life into all that clay. She even, sometimes, told herself that if she could look honestly at Cynthia she might find her a bit of a lout. She decided that if you couldn't be with the person you wanted to be with, it was best to be alone. The dream was the life she had chosen. She saw herself in every other old maid drifting out on a white, formless sea.

> Who, ere he make one,
> With millions toyeth,
> And lightly destroyeth
> Whate'er is begun.

Bernie was not one such. Bernie was big and bearlike and scruffy, booming her demands across the library, richly self-absorbed: no doubt in Bernie's mind but that any stone idol she built would be the model for every future production of *Nabucco*; the library was instantly to deliver reproductions of every feeble antecedent. This the librarian did, with scarcely a sign of mockery. Bernie was also touchingly, clumsily chivalrous, flinging open doors, looming up behind to reach the high shelves, offering lifts home in her rattletrap truck on nights when the bus stop was a cold wet wait. There was surely no need for Bernie to be at the library every day? What could this vigorous woman want from an old maid?

But Bernie did want. And an old maid knew too well what Bernie was going through, and she didn't have the heart to say No for very long.

So she said Yes, and took some of the happiness that flowed out of Bernie. She was grateful to Bernie for being big and butch and having enough passion for two and not noticing that anything was missing. She loved the garden and stone-dusty little house, nowadays much coveted by estate agents, which Bernie had picked up cheap from an elderly lover of sculpture.

As the years passed and Bernie never tired of fingering at the mysteriousness she found in her lover, she came to know her secret as a poor but potent thing. Sometimes, in the long winter evenings, while Bernie chipped away (Bernie was always working) and she crouched over the fire, sorting out crocus bulbs for planting under the rowan tree, she moved Cynthia out of her mind to marvel at the undiminished brightness of Bernie's passion. But would Bernie love her so much if Bernie were able to possess her? Did her secret vice make a living space for Bernie's virtue? But these were unworthy thoughts: Bernie believed, like a child, in goodness.

And when she cried when they were together it was not always for Cynthia; sometimes it was for the shame of deceit; sometimes it was for Bernie, who deserved better than a wraith.

> Nay, thee, Love, he gave
> His terrors to cover,
> And turn to a lover
> His insolent slave.

'Ready to model now, flower?'

As she seated herself in the chair placed for her in the studio, Bernie gently pushed back her hair. 'How will I ever capture the Magdalen's little ear?' Bernie's stone-gritty fingers felt along the curves. 'You know, petal, if I was half the artist I love you enough to be I could make this ear would hear twice as much as van der Weyden's "Magdalen Reading". Just stay for me a minute.'

For a minute? If she could give one whole minute, she would be able to give a life.

Rogier van der Weyden's Magdalen Reading *is in the National Gallery, London. Unlike many later representations of the Magdalen, it shows her not as a repenting whore but a virginal young woman, reading from a devotional book and listening to a voice from another world.*

Gustav Holst's Six Songs from Robert Bridges *are written for women's voices.*

SHEBA publishes a wide range of books by women. A selection of our forthcoming and recent titles is listed below. You can buy SHEBA books from any good bookshop or order them direct. Just send a cheque or postal order, including 75p p&p for each book ordered, to SHEBA FEMINIST PUBLISHERS, 10A BRADBURY STREET, LONDON N16 8JN. Or call 071-254 1590 for our free catalogue.

FICTION

The Move
by Tina Kendall
First novel by young black novelist: the heroine's search for herself takes her to Africa and beyond.
£5.99 ISBN 0 907179 46 0
Available: June 1991

People in Trouble
by Sarah Schulman
A novel about AIDS and the impact it has on all our lives from a woman's perspective.
£5.99 ISBN 0 907179 53 3
Available: Now

The Sophie Horowitz Story
by Sarah Schulman
First novel about an intrepid feminist reporter about to take on more than she bargained for.
£5.99 ISBN 0 907179 54 1
Available: April 1991

Ghost Pains
by Jane Severance
A grown up novel about growing up. Alcohol and its disturbing effects threaten the world of two teenage sisters.
£5.99 ISBN 0 907179 45 2
Available: May 1991

Excitement:
Sexual Stories for the 90s
Eds: The Sheba Collective
With heterosexual, bi-sexual and lesbian heroines, this collection is risque, daring, and, above all, exciting.
£6.99 ISBN: 0 907179 57 6
Available: October 1991

More Serious Pleasure
Eds. The Sheba Collective
A second volume of lesbian erotic stories and poems. If the first volume left you hot, read this one!
£6.99 ISBN: 0 907179 52 5
Available: Now

NON-FICTION
Through the Break
Eds. Pearlie McNeill, Marie McShea & Pratibha Parmar
This successful collection of women's testimonies of survival is back in print. Valuable for personal reading as well as a useful resource guide.
£7.99 ISBN 0 907179 39 8
Available: May 1991